Flowers of York

C J Lock

Copyright © 2017 C J Lock

All rights reserved.

ISBN: 9781521476741

DEDICATION

To the illegitimate children of Richard Plantagenet, Duke of Gloucester, later King Richard III. Your dates of birth and death are unknown, but you are not forgotten.

Table of Contents

The Rose 7
The Sword 15
The Falcon 22
The Ribbon 29
The Rosary 34
The Innocent 40
The Lamb 45
The Cross 52
Epilogue 60
AUTHOR'S NOTES 61

ACKNOWLEDGMENTS

As usual my thanks go to all my friends who constantly support my continuing efforts. Without their encouragement and honest words, I never would have dared to write my first, never mind this, my fifth book! Special thanks as usual to Amanda, my tenacious proof reader, for her hard work and endless patience in correcting the many errors caused by my brain overtaking my fingers. And thanks to Charlotte – whose approach to me for help on her project caused the idea of this book to bloom...

Foreword

We have all, at one time, experienced the promise of youth. Maybe, even felt one defining moment when the whole world of possibilities opened up before us. Times may change, years may have passed, but I don't doubt that emotions were still the same in medieval times, when such ambitions could be snuffed out like a candle, and often were. You may have been born at the wrong time, into the wrong family. Pinned your colours to the wrong mast. What was then the 'Wheel of Fortune.'
These eight stories focus on a flowering of youth that was to be pruned short. Young children who should have had so much to live for, born into lives of power and privilege. But in that very birth, was the genesis of their demise.
We only know the date of birth and death of two of these children, but they all remain enigmatic figures. Names on ancient manuscripts, bright flashes of colour on an illuminated page.
Too often the spotlight falls on two other children, their fates endlessly debated time and time again. They also paid a price for the nature of their birth, but what price? No one really knows. Yes, undoubtedly they died at some time, but when, where and why will remain a secret. At least until some day, in some dusty archive, when a hand will reach out and turn over the document that reveals the truth. It has to be somewhere. Someone must have known what happened.
Life is precious. Like a beautiful flower it flourishes in the sun, heads held high forever towards the light. Some hold on for a season, gradually wilting, petals dappling the ground one by one. Others share a different fate. Fingers reach out and pluck at their stems, snap them in half, casting their promise to the four winds. Such was the fate of these Flowers of York.

I hope you can sense their presence in the fragrance as you wander by.

The Rose
July 1476

I know Mama is sad, and I have had to hide my excitement from her. Which has meant trying to hide it from myself, so that she could not see how happy I was.

Not that I ever wanted to leave her, far from it. I wish she could have come with us. I asked Alice if she could, but she just smiled and said it was not possible. I like Alice, she is kind, and always tells me how pretty I am. How I have my father's colouring. I don't think I do. I think my brother John looks much more like him than I do. But John is very sad today, as he did not want to leave. He wanted to stay with Mama and not go to my father's castle of Middleham, where he will be trained to be a knight. How can he not be excited? But he is only small, and I have to remember that and take good care of him.

We are riding over the drawbridge now, and I am pleased to finally be here. The castle is tall and square, dark and grey. It stands sturdily in the ground, not like Pontefract Castle, which rambles over the slope and tumbles down to the village. The sunlight bounces off a stained glass window above me, and I look up and see my father's banner fluttering in the breeze. The white boar, on a field of murrey and blue. It makes me feel proud. Is that silly? That I am proud to be the daughter of the king's brother? I don't care if it does, not really. When I am older I will tell everyone that my father is a powerful man and they will be full of envy. I know he is admired by many people for my Mama would not love him as she does if he were not a good man.

My father is not here today. He has gone south and he is also very sad.

His own father and brother were killed in a battle long ago. The king has now asked him to take their bodies to be buried in the place where they would wish to rest in eternal peace. Not in the place where they were killed so cruelly. It is a place called Fotheringhay. It is where my father was born and I hope I am able to go there one day. I cannot imagine what it would be like to lose my father and my brother. I cannot think of it. My father was only seven when it happened. That is my age now.

Alice holds my hand tightly after we dismount, and I see many servants stopping, or slowing down, to look at us as we stand by the stairs which lead up into the massive keep. They seem curious, one or two of them smile and seem friendly. John huddles close to my skirts, and I put my hand out to comfort him, cupping his cheek. He pushes closer to me. He has never been outside of Pontefract and so this must be frightening for him. It is a strange place today, but will soon become our home. We have nothing to be afraid of here, I know my father will see to that.

A man with a rough, bushy beard waits at the bottom of the covered staircase and nods politely to Alice. He is very tall. I almost squint to look up at him.

"Mistress Burgh, Her Grace awaits you in the Great Chamber. Your chests will be sent up to your rooms in the guest apartments." He smiles at me, briefly. Alice inclines her head politely.

"Thank you, Sir John." She says in her usual clipped tones. Everything about Alice is neat and precise. I think I drive her mad with my untidy ways. I will have to try harder, now I am here. I have to be grown up now. I have to become a lady.

Sir John turns on his heel and we follow him up the stairs, past a guardhouse, and onwards, up even more stairs. At the top, we pass a chapel. I smell incense and through an open door I see a rainbow of colours filtering through a window on shards of light. But then we move on, across a great hall. A table sits at one end on a small raised dais, chairs arranged in front of a banner, once again displaying the white boar and the white rose which is our house. Or, one of our houses.

My Mama told me tales of our Irish ancestors. Of the Fitzgerald family, of the Earls of Desmond. It gives me a strange feeling inside to think that I have family there too! On an island across the sea. It sounds a truly wonderful place and know that Mama was very sad to leave. Until she met my father.

Alice leads us through a door and my eyes are immediately drawn to a large window embrasure which takes up most of the room. There are two women seated there, their chairs sitting on a dais reached by three steps. One of them is sewing, the other has her head bent over a book. I look up at Alice, suddenly feeling terribly nervous. I so wanted to be here, but now... with these strangers? What will they think of me? What if they don't like me? What if I don't like them?

John is looking around, his eyes wide, taking in a large tapestry which shows knights on horseback. I think they are the knights of King Arthur, and their armour shimmers with gold thread in the sunlight.

The women look up.

One of them is quite young and has blue eyes. Bright, like speedwell. She gives me a shy smile and she is very pretty. The older lady does not move for a moment, but then she sits back and closes the book before her on the table. As if she has just finished a page. I wonder if she has heard us enter, she is so still, but then she rises gracefully from her seat. She turns towards us, and moves slowly down the steps. I hold my breath as she comes closer.

This must be the Lady Anne. Our Father's wife. She is dressed in a gown of pink silk, the sleeves and bodice tipped with green velvet. Her hair is the colour of birch-bark, and to me, she looks as delicate as a rose. And just as fair. She is as different from Mama as spring is from autumn. Cool, and fresh as morning dew, whereas Mama is warm. A wild, tawny, tumbled beauty.

Alice nudges me sharply and I curtsey, following her lead, as Lady Anne halts before us. Oh I do hope she doesn't hate us! But as I rise from my curtsey, her eyes alight on John, and for a moment she looks sad. For just one moment, before she looks back at me and smiles.

"Well, Alice." Lady Anne speaks very softly. "Who do we have here?" Alice draws up her shoulders a little. She is only slightly taller than I am.

"Your Grace, this is Kathryn, and her brother John."

Lady Anne looks back at John again. Does she not like me? I watch, worried, as she lowers herself down to look more closely at my brother, who pushes himself into the folds of Alice's skirts. He can be so shy, and he is still very young. I want to tell her so but dare not speak.

"Do you like marchpane John?" John turns up his dark grey eyes to look at me. I smile and nod. He copies me, instantly, fixing his gaze on Lady Anne. She looks pleased and I am relieved. "Hob has made some especially for you. It is in the nursery. Would you like some?" This time he does not look at me, emerging slightly from the cocoon he has made for himself. Mama always says he has a sweet tooth! He nods willingly now, smiling himself as Lady Anne rises up once more.

"Alice, would you take John to the nursery?" She pauses, strangely I feel. "Edward is there to greet him."

Alice curtseys in agreement and takes John's hand. Suddenly, I am left alone, watching them leave through a door on the other side of the room. Leaving me standing, wondering what I am to do. But then she speaks again, holding out her hand towards the window.

"Kathryn, this is Lady Lovell."

The girl looks up at me from her place at the table, and I give another quick curtsey. Lord Lovell is my father's friend but I did not know his sister was at Middleham. He is quite serious and I like to try and make him smile. He has a lovely smile. I remember when I was much younger, and he would sit me on his knee and play the lute. The memory pleases me and makes me feel happy. Lady Lovell smiles back at me. I hope she will be my friend. I have not had a friend before. Most of my time was spent with Mama. Unless I could sneak off into the kitchens and talk to the servants, which I often tried to do. There was a young girl there, called Mary. She used to stir the pot.

"Come," Lady Anne says gently, "come and sit with us. You must be tired after your journey."

I am not tired. What I want more than anything is to remove my shoes and feel the smooth, cool stone under my feet. I do not know why, but having my feet trussed up like a fowl makes me feel uncomfortable. I scrunch my toes together unconsciously. My feet agree! Only for now, here, I need to behave. I must not shame Mama. I will no longer be able to wander around the passages and halls bare-foot. My father calls me a hoyden when he catches me, but it makes him laugh. I love to hear him laugh. His eyes crinkle and it make me feel very special to him.

I step up to the window seat and sit down carefully, aware that both ladies are watching me closely.

"I am very pleased to meet you, Kathryn." Lady Lovell has a very sweet voice.

"Thank you, my lady." I reply. I am nervous now. I do not know what I should do. I did not expect to spend time with Lady Anne. She is far too grand a lady to waste time on me. I thought I would just be shown to my chamber, before being told what to do and where to go. I knew where the chapel was now. Do I eat in the Great Hall, or is there somewhere else I have to go? I am not at Pontefract anymore. Mama was there, so I always knew my place.

"My name is Anna," Lady Lovell smiles. Somehow I think she knows how I feel. I clasp my fingers together tightly in the folds of my skirts. I wish John was here. Maybe they would pay less attention to me if he was still here, as he is such a cherub. He managed to melt everyone's heart back at home. Especially Lady Maude, who has no children of her own.

I cannot think of anything to say. I bite my lip. Maybe if I am quiet they will let me retire.

"Anna." The Lady Anne speaks up suddenly and it makes me jump. I am not used to feeling this nervous and suddenly I do wish I was back at home. Anna's eyes are wide and fringed with gold, not at all like her brothers. "Would you go to the nursery and see how John and Edward are getting along. I am sure we need not tire his new companion for too long and I would like him to meet... Kathryn."

Anna doesn't speak at all but merely nods, puts her needlework down on the table and slips away. Anne watches her go, her face is thoughtful.

"Poor child. To be married so young."

"Married?" I cannot help my curiosity. I hope I have not spoken out of turn and I blush a little. But Lady Anne does not seem to mind.

"Why, yes. You have met Francis, her husband? I assumed you have because he visits Pontefract often with the duke."

My own eyes must have expressed the confusion I was feeling. Anna – Lord Lovell's wife? Surely, she was half his age?

Anne nods at me, hearing my question without me having to speak a word.

"They were married when she was but six years old." She turns her head then; her profile catches the light. She is very fair and I feel large and ungainly sitting next to her. Surely she must notice? My hands grip each other tighter. "I think it has been difficult for both of them."

Now we are alone, I feel a little braver. Not so worried that I may say or do the wrong thing. Lady Anne seems kind, and I feel sure she will forgive my questions. At least I hope she will. There are so many things I want to know.

"But, my Mama tells me that you and Papa were..." I stop suddenly. Her face seems to tighten within my first few words. What have I said? She closes her eyes for a moment, as I try to think what I may have done wrong. All I was going to say is that I had been told that the Lady Anne and father were friends from a young age, and they still married. Although, now it makes sense to me. They were both of the right age when they wed. Anna's husband would have been twice her age, at least. Lady Anne is looking at me again, eyes clear as a woodland stream. There is a look behind her eyes which I do not understand.

"How is your Mama?" She tries to smile, but does not quite manage it and turns back to the window. "I have not seen her for such a long time." Her fingers toy with the gold band on her finger. "Not since before you were born." It pleases me that she has mentioned Mama. Mama warned me that she may not do so, even though at one time they were friends.

"She is very well," I reply, for it is true. "She reads a lot, and has Lady Maude for company. Although she was very sad when we left to come here." For the first time, I feel a pang of guilt. "I hope she will not be too lonely now we have gone."

"It is a terrible thing to lose your children," she replies gently, "but she knows you will be well looked after under our care." This concern for Mama cheers me greatly and I smile happily.

"Oh yes! I know she loves our father so much! She told us he will turn John into a gallant knight and myself into a lady of the court."

Once again her face grows a little sad. I do not like that I have made her sad. Her eyes are downcast.

"Well, one of my ladies at the very least. We do not often travel to court. Although we may go for the holy season, if the king desires it."

My heart leaps into my mouth. Christmas! In London at the king's court! I had never thought! The fine ladies, their dresses and jewels! I only know of it from what Mama has told me, and I cannot wait to see it for myself. I long to hear the music and dance with a handsome lord. Maybe, even..? I stop my racing thoughts, feeling my cheeks go warm at the thought of a husband for myself. I do not want a husband. Not yet. Not to be wed as Anna is to a man I do not know. Lady Anne picks up on my change of mood as quickly as Mama would.

"What is it?" But she is not Mama. She is Lady Anne. She is my father's wife. Like him she is of noble blood, a royal cousin.

"I..." I cannot bring myself to say more.

Her face softens. She reaches out, unexpectedly, and touches my cheek.

"Speak, child. For I must become your mother now that you are here under our roof. The duke expects no less and I want you to feel happy to come and talk to me about anything which troubles you."

She seems so kind and gentle. As she drops her hand I sense a fragrance which is not familiar to me, but is sweet and heady. Like a summer garden.

"Mama told me that I will become a lady here and will one day marry."

Anne smiles, and nods her head.

"You will. But only when the time is right." She laughs then right prettily as she catches the relief which washes over me. "I take it that as far as you are concerned you are happy to wait?" I nod, perhaps too enthusiastically. "Then that is what you and I shall work on together, shall we?" Her assent to my wishes makes me smile even broader, apart from one small worry that nags at my stomach.

"But, fa... the duke?"

Lady Anne takes my hand then, looks at my fingers, as if examining them one by one. Mama says I have father's hands. Long and slim fingered.

"Don't worry about the duke. I will tell him that first there is much you should accomplish and he will listen to my counsel. Now tell me, what is it you like to do?" She keeps my hand in hers and I have to admit it makes me feel comforted.

"Well," I answer carefully, "I like to dance, and to ride. I think I would also like to hunt. I would like my own falcon and maybe a puppy to grow into a faithful dog. I would like to learn how to use a longbow. And a horse. I would very much like my own horse."

Now she is laughing with me, and her fingers close over mine, gently.

"Do you know, I think if I were to ask my son the same question when he is your age, he will ask for exactly the same things." Her nose wrinkles. 'Well, maybe not so much the dancing!" She pauses then, her eyes now sparkling merrily. She seems a lot happier than when I came into the room earlier. As if we are now friends. If ever I can call my father's wife a friend. Would that be right? I would really like that if I could. "And, is there anything you don't like?"

"Sewing, Latin, Scripture." I answer so quickly my face burns at my own honesty, but I see the amusement in her face. She pats my hand, finally releasing my fingers. I miss her warmth immediately.

"Ah, well. I feel we may have to strike a bargain. In return for attending to the things you do not like, I am sure we can attain some of the things you desire. What do you say to that?"

It is then I remember something I have forgotten to add. But it is important.

"I don't like shoes much either."

Lady Anne sits back against the cushions and folds her hands in her lap. She is now looking at me almost fondly. In the same way father does.

"Strangely enough, I have already been told that."

"Really?" I cannot stifle my surprise, knowing I have raised my brows. She laughs again.

"The duke told me. He also told me I would find you most engaging. And I find that he was right." Engaging? I am a little taken aback by the word, but it seems to have pleased her so I smile. "Well then," she says, her eyes still brightly sparkling. "We must get you settled in." She pauses, and sits forwards. "Just one more thing."

"Yes, Your Grace?"

She clears her throat. She seems a little nervous herself, which makes me frown.

"Write to your mother often. The duke sends letters to Pontefract and yours can go at the same time. Ensure she knows how you attend to your lessons, and assure her that you are growing into the fine young lady she wishes you to be."

I nod, for what she says is no hardship and will make Mama feel happy. It is only then I remember some of Mama's last words to me.

"Lady Anne?"

"Yes, child?" Her hand reaches up and touches my hair, light as a feather.

"Do you wish me to try not to talk about Mama, whilst I am in your home? Mama said... she said I had to have a care not to offend you."

Before I can do anything else, she reaches over and cups my face with her hands. Her voice is low, almost a whisper.

"My dear Kathryn! What passed between your Mama and the duke happened a long time ago. I bear her no ill will, nor her children either. You are welcome here. I want you to know that. Truly!"

There is a noise by the door as it opens, and Anna reappears, smiling. She is holding a young, fair-haired child on her hip. He is small, smaller than my brother John, but he is fair of face, and has Lady Anne's eyes. As he sees her, he reaches out his arms and makes a gurgling noise which is both as amusing as it is hard to understand.

Lady Anne rises, her face transformed, her eyes full of love. I have seen that before. In my own Mama's eyes.

"Ah, thank you, Anna." She takes the child, and settles him on her knee, as Anna comes to stand beside me. Lady Anne's voice is full of love and pride. "Kathryn, this is my son. Our very own, Rose of York. Meet your brother Edward."

My eyes meet his dove grey ones and he smiles at me. I have another brother and my heart soars. I will live with my father and the Lady Anne, and I know I will be very happy here.

The Sword
September 1482

My nurse in very annoyed with me. I was so excited yesterday that I paid scarce attention to my Latin text, ate very little food and kept a constant watch at the window, waiting for the hour Papa would return home. From my tower chamber in the castle I can see far into the north and my father was due to return any hour. He has been away in the savage borderlands, where the wild-haired Scotsmen and their wolves ravage the border, setting fire to villages, and stealing cattle.

My brother John says I am wrong about the wolves, but I think it is he who is wrong. My father showed me a map once, and it said that there be wolves there, roaming free!

I love my brother John very much but I think I annoy him too sometimes. Then other times we are as bad as each other and tease our sister Kathryn. One day we found a frog down by the riverside, and hid it in her coffer. She was not frightened as other girls would be. She was angry though, as we had put it on her best gown. She picked up the frog and chased John around the bailey, trying to pull his collar down and slip the poor thing down his jerkin!

I was pleased that the frog escaped in the end. Poor thing!

John then wanted to mix a bowl of orange-flower water with horse-piss for when Kathryn next washed her hair, but I dare not help him do that. Even though we laughed about it. John laughed a lot. They have a different mother to me, but they both live here at the castle, and Papa treats us all the same. I am pleased, because Mama has no other children, and so if they were not here, I would be alone, and I think I would be lonely.

Papa came home after I was put to bed, so in the end I did not see him until chapel this morning, but he remembered!

So, now we wait in the bailey and the sun has come out. I see John come from the stairway at the bottom of the keep, and I wave to him. But Mama follows him out, and she does not look at all pleased. That saddens me, for she has a beautiful smile, and I wish she would smile all of the time. I make her sad sometimes, I think. But I try not to. I try really hard! It is worse when I am not well. On the days when I become really hot, and sick, and cannot rise from my bed. Sometimes, I don't even remember becoming ill. I feel strange, and begin to shake. Then I wake up in my bed, feeling very tired. As if I had not been to bed at all! Mistress Idley tells me I must not get over-excited. But today, I cannot help it. So, of course she is annoyed with me, and I am guessing my Mama is too.

For today, Papa will keep his promise. Today he will let me ride his very own horse, White Surrey. Only around the bailey, that is true. But today, instead of my pied palfrey, Minerva, who is mild and gentle of step, I will sit upon a true war-horse, and see the world as Papa sees it. I am so excited I can hardly breathe! Then I feel Mama's hand upon my shoulder, and I look up.

"Edward, Mistress Idley tells me you did not eat breakfast."

That was true. I am so happy I cannot eat a thing.

"What's happening?" John asks, looking at me as Mama shakes her head.

I am about to answer when Papa appears, leading White Surrey through the east gatehouse and I catch my breath. I hear John do the same. We have seen him many times, but today somehow he seems different. Larger, more majestic. His mane and tail are the same colour as storm clouds. He looks like a horse born for a king! To me, at least.

He is already saddled, with Papa's red leather saddle, and I watch as he leads him over to a mounting block. Servants have begun to emerge from the kitchen and bake-house, and I can see Sir John, the Steward, standing by the gate with a grin on his face. Suddenly, I begin to feel a bit nervous.

Mama moves forwards quickly, and lays her hand on Papa's arm.

"Richard, is this wise? If he should fall..."

Papa smiles back, and passes his hand down Surrey's neck. The animal gives a small whinny in response, shaking his head, proudly. As if he has heard Mama and he does not agree with her.

"Dearest, don't fret. Surrey will look after him, and I will be here at his side. He will come to no harm." He then leans forward, as if to kiss her, but instead he whispers something in her ear and they both look at me. I do not hear what he says, but he holds out his hand to me. I hear John gasp.

"Are you going to ride him?"

But I am already walking forwards. Papa takes my hand and I step up onto the mounting block. Mama steps back, but Papa is still smiling, his dark hair shining in the sunlight.

"Slow and careful as you mount," he murmurs to me so no one can hear. "Sit well back in the saddle, straight and square, as you were taught. Surrey will do the rest."

The stirrup has already been shortened and I put my foot onto the bar, launching myself up, and throwing my leg over Surrey's haunches. I land in the saddle, feel its padded protection beneath me. I am so high! Even though Surrey is not that much taller than Minerva, it seems as if I am on the very top of the highest battlement. I hold my breath, taking up the reins in my hand, feeling Surrey pull on the bit, he shakes his head once more.

Papa moves in as Will, the stable-hand, moves the block away. He adjusts the stirrup again, checking the girth with brows knotted. His hands work fast and sure. Then he moves away from me and I am alone, seated on White Surrey for a second as if he were my very own. I sit up even straighter and look around. I can see John, his face full of awe. Then Papa places his hand on my right foot, and adjusts that stirrup too. He pats my calf gently and I look down upon him. He is smiling.

"Are you ready?"

I nod, unable to speak. I can feel the power beneath me. Feel that Surrey wants to run and gallop. Wants to feel the wind in his mane and tail, streaming out behind him like a banner. Like Papa's banner! I imagine myself in armour, sitting at the head of a large army. Ready to fight for my country. To fight for my uncle, the king. Papa speaks again.

"We will walk around the keep to the chapel and back to this spot. Keep the reins high, but light. He doesn't like his head to be too controlled. Do you understand?"

I nod again. I know many people are watching me. The whole of the castle seems to have come to a standstill. But I dare not look at anyone. I have to concentrate, very hard. I don't want to let Papa down.

"Very well," he says again quietly, his eyes fixed on mine. "Walk him on."

Swallowing hard, I touch my heels to the silver flanks, feeling the taut muscles there. Obediently, Surrey steps forwards, on towards the north range. This is nothing like riding my palfrey! She ambles along at a steady pace but this is different. I can feel it as Surrey raises his hooves higher, steps out, forcing me to remain upright, control my balance with my thighs. My muscles are weak, and it makes them ache, but I will not fail. I feel as if my head is on a level with the sky! The ground a mile away beneath my feet as we round the corner, pass the rooms where the scribes and clerks of the estate work studiously, pens scratching on parchment, attending to the affairs of the castle.

I can see the tower here my chamber is. I can almost see into the window of my room! I begin to relax, see my father nodding and smiling as he passes the servants who have come out to watch us. He looks so proud. His guiding hand remaining on the bridle. Just in case.

We turn by the chapel and retrace our steps. Everyone is still smiling and I feel much easier in the saddle. I sorely want to dig my heels into Surrey's flanks, to feel the wind in my hair too! To fly out through the east gate, across the outer bailey and down to the river. Dare I?

My legs prepare to kick back when suddenly Papa speaks.

"Pull him up, Ned."

I obey, tugging back on the reins. Surrey lowers his head and we come to a halt. We are back at the keep stairs, and my mother smiles. Relieved.

John is still there, and now Lord Lovell is at his side. They stand with Sir Robert Percy. Everyone is happy. Lord Lovell claps his hands, and Sir Robert joins in. So does Sir John. Only my brother looks sad. No, not sad. I don't know how he looks. But he is not smiling. Lord Lovell leans down and speaks to him, and then his lips do curve. Just a little. He bites the inside of his cheek, like Papa does. Now and then.

Papa looks up at me.

"Can you dismount or do you want the block?"

I look down at the ground. Everyone is still watching and I desperately want to kick my foot from the stirrup and slide myself down to the floor. How I have done many times. To dismount like a knight would, with ease and elegance. As I have seen Papa do, many times. But Surrey seems so much taller! Papa senses my uncertainty, I know he does, but he does not try to stop me. I know that he wants me to do it as much I as I do. But I am afraid. All these people are watching and if I fall...

"Richard!"

Mama's voice rings out in warning across the bailey and Papa turns. Will is scurrying towards us, carrying the block.

"Never mind." Papa whispers, looking back at me, his hand resting on my thigh. "Maybe another time." But I see the disappointment in his eyes, and I cannot bear it. I am his son, and want him to be proud of me, and one day he will. I am sure of it. I dismount, get both feet onto the block and my eyes fall upon John as he talks to Sir Robert. I have an idea. If Papa allows it.

He takes my hand as I stand on the top of the block, and helps me step down. I hope he will understand.

"Papa?"

He looks down at me, his hand ruffles my hair.

"Well done, Ned. You sat him very well! You will make a great knight one day."

I swallow hard and turn to pat Surrey's neck in thanks.

"Papa, I bet John can ride him. He is older and stronger than me. Can John ride too?"

He looks at me in surprise, his brow knots. Then, he glances over at John, and I see he understands. When he looks back at me I see the pride in his face.

"John?"

Everyone looks up as Papa calls over to my brother. John raises his head. I can't help but call to him too.

"It is your turn John! Come! Come and ride White Surrey?"

Everyone stops. Mama looks surprised. She looks at me, then John, who has not moved. It seems to have gone very quiet.

"Go on, John!" Lord Lovell says, suddenly loud. "If you don't, I will. I have been dying to ride that horse for years and His Grace would never let me near!"

Papa grins and John smiles broadly.

"May I?" he asks hesitantly.

Papa nods and John walks over. I feel so excited for him. Almost as excited as I have been for myself.

"He won't need the block Papa!"

After a second, Papa motions Will to take the mounting block away, and he leans forwards, cupping his hands together, like any normal squire. This even shocks me, and as I look around, I can see I am not alone. But John is braver, taller and stronger than me, and without hesitation, he launches himself up into the saddle, as if he has done it every day of his life.

Papa re-adjusts the stirrups, and as I step back, I see him say something to John, who is nodding, taking the reins into his hands. Surrey snorts, sensing his change of rider. His hooves paw the ground. Papa runs his hand down Surrey's muzzle, as if he understands what he has to do. Then Papa steps back. I know what is about to happen and I don't know how I feel. Until I see Papa's face.

John flicks his heels backwards, and Surrey charges forwards into a canter. He has wanted his head, and John has the strength and skill that I do not. He is older than me. And stronger.

Many people watch and clap their hands. John rounds the keep then takes a left over to the east gate, charging out of our sight, into the outer bailey. We hear the shouts and cheers of the grooms and servants as he rides White Surrey round past the stables, the laundry and the smithy. Papa turns to Lord Lovell and Sir Robert and they all grin at each other, but Papa's smile fades first.

We cannot see John, but I hear the pounding of hooves getting closer. He returns across the bridge, pulls hard on the reins as he reaches us. Surrey halts immediately and snorts in satisfaction, I think. John's cheeks are bright red; he smiles fit to bust. I am so proud of my brother, if a little jealous of his skill. But not for long. For he helps me every day, and soon I will be as good a rider as him. I know I will!

John dismounts as Papa crosses over to him, and they both greet each other, smiling. I turn to look for Mama, but she is no longer here.

Everyone returns to their chores, and I watch as Surrey is led away. I feel a pang of regret that I cannot get back on him again. I watch his tail swish lazily and John smiles at me as Lord Lovell puts an arm around his shoulder. I grin back. Papa walks towards me and for the moment I stay silent.

"Come with me," he says softly, and I wonder if I have displeased him, as he now appears far too serious. I thought he was pleased, to see John ride White Surrey so well. I was sorry that Mama missed it. Maybe she had been called away by one of her ladies. She always has so much to do.

I follow Papa up the stairs and across the hall. Then across the covered bridge and into his privy chamber. I don't see Mama anywhere, there is only one of Papa's hounds. Tristan. Curled before the fire, still sleeping.

I wait. I have been in his chamber many times. It is where Papa keeps his books and one of his many chess sets. Lord Lovell often sits and talks with him here, late into the night. Now Papa has something in his hand, which he has taken from a chest by the wall. It is wrapped in crimson velvet. It is faded, as if it is old. Papa sits down on the chair in front of me so his face is level with mine.

"Edward, that was very generous of you. You have made me very proud today."

I shrug, trying not so betray how pleased I am. Papa is sparing in his praise. It has to be earned. Today I did so, easily.

"I knew John would be able to ride him. And I know I will be as good as him one day. When I grow older."

Papa nods, serious.

"You will. I am sure of it. But today you showed everyone how grown up you can be. How generous and fair. These are qualities that are important in a prince of the royal blood, and you have shown yourself to be cognisant of this. Everyone here will have marked that well." He raises his hands. I think I know what is inside the velvet. My throat feels dry. "Today, you have proved yourself to be a true prince of York. I was waiting to give this to you in a year or so, but you have earned it now."

He holds it out to me, draws back the velvet. There, balanced on his hands, is the most magnificent sword I have ever seen. Slowly, he draws it from its sheath of engraved silver, and hands me the blade, hilt first. The grip is in the shape of a dappled falcon, with gold claws and rubies for eyes.

"Papa! I don't deserve this!" I gasp "I did not do anything!"

Although I do want to take the sword from his hand, I can't. He is wrong! I have not done anything. He only gave me what I desired. The chance to ride a war-horse. Papa sighs gently. Hs eyes crease at the corners.

"My son, you have shown everyone here in your home what a great prince you will be one day. John is my bastard son. I love and care for him all too well, but you are my heir. You are the one who will one day inherit all I possess and more. John will always be in your shadow, no matter what rewards I can give to him. Today, you assured me that you will take care of him, no matter what happens to me."

Suddenly I was frightened out of my wits. Was he ill? Was he off to battle? Was there trouble with the Scots?

I dare not ask, but I take the sword from his hand with care, hold it to the light, let it glance down the blade. It feels comfortable in my hand, despite how deadly the blade looks.

Papa sits back in his chair.

"It belonged to my father, your grandsire. He gave it to me when I was a little younger than you are now. I still remember it. At Ludlow. Before he rode off to his castle in Wakefield. It was the last time I saw him." There are tears in his eyes, I am sure, as he takes the sword from me and slides it back into its sheath. The metal makes a satisfying slithering sound. He passes it to me again and I take it from him. My very own sword. My grandfather's sword. I can hardly speak.

Papa is looking at me and his eyes are shining. He smiles. A different smile. Carefully, I place the sword beside me on the floor and stand up.

"Thank you Papa," I say softly. He nods, his lips press together, as if he cannot speak and I know he is thinking of his own Papa. I cannot bear to see him unhappy. I know I am too old now, but I step towards him. "I love you very much!"

I wrap my arms around his neck and he envelops me in his embrace, pulling me closer to him. His face nuzzles into my neck. I can smell soap and costmary. It is like I am a very young boy again. I feel safe. Nothing can ever harm me or hurt me. Never. Papa is strong, and he will not allow it. I smile into his hair as he whispers in my ear, the sword forgotten.

"Edward, my beloved son. You are my very heart!"

The Falcon
April 1483

The sakker swoops down out of a cloudless sky, almost skimming the grasses before it lands on Lord Lovell's outstretched hand. He grins in satisfaction and turns towards me.

"See?"

I like Lord Lovell a lot. He has smiling, deep brown eyes and dark golden hair. He is Papa's closest friend. It could have been hard when my sister and I came here from our home in Pontefract Castle. We had to leave our mother and come here to live with our other family. I was only young, and don't remember too much at first. But my sister is older, and she tells me that he looked after her. That whenever she was sad, or angry, he seemed to be there.

I was pleased that we were going hunting. Papa had been laughing with us, before we left the castle. He has business to attend to and could not join us. He wagered Lord Lovell's falcon would fly away and end up in York. I did not understand the jest, but my father leaned over to me and whispered in my ear.

"Ask him about Lark!"

Lord Lovell had laughed too and shook his head.

I look proudly at my own bird. A Lanner Falcon. Yesterday was my name day and Papa gave me the beautiful, cream breasted bird which now balanced on my hand. It was the bird given to Esquires to fly. I am no esquire. No Lord either. I still find it hard to believe that I had been given such a gift.

"What will you call him?" asks Lord Lovell. I purse my lips and look at the sky. I already know.

"Lir."

I see him start, his brow creases which makes me smile. I knew it would surprise him.

"Lir? That is indeed a strange name."

I stroke my bird's breast gently, it's hazel eyes are shiny and alert. Like rain washed stone.

"Lir is the Irish God of the sea." I tell him of the story my Mama used to tell me, one of the many tales from the land of her birth. How Lir married Aoife, and she grew jealous of his children, turning them into swans. That is how they lived for nine hundred years until St Patrick came to Ireland and released them from their curse. As I finish my tale, Lord Lovell looks at me strangely. I think he has tears in his eyes. That he looks unhappy, but he smiles.

"It is a fine name. Even for a bird that may never see the sea that is his domain."

I smile at him, as Lir stretches out his wings.

"But when he flies, he may see swans. He may see his children!"

We turn back towards the castle, and before long are riding through the outer bailey. The noise of a horse, thundering across the ground, comes up behind us, and Lord Lovell looks around, concerned. It is a rider, his courser lathered with sweat and foam. Lord Lovell hands his bird to a waiting squire and dismounts quickly, as the messenger's horse skids to a halt, legs rearing frantically.

As the rider finds his feet, Lord Lovell is beside him. The man wears a Black Bull badge. I do not know whose badge that is, but the man falls to his knees, and hands over a letter.

I do not think anything of it. Messages arrive all the time from towns all over Yorkshire, and often from London. From the king to his brother.

Another squire takes Lir from my hand, and after I dismount, I want to take him back, want to walk him into the mews myself. But something stops me and I look back.

Lord Lovell looks at the letter and his face turns goes as white as milk. He turns his back on the rider and strides towards the eastern gatehouse, disappearing into the inner bailey. The rider stares after him. It is not like Lord Lovell not to offer riders our hospitality! He is moving quickly, but I follow him, keeping my distance in case he should hear me and tell me to stay behind. I don't know why I feel I need to find out what is happening, but I do.

I trail him up the stairs, past the chapel and across the great hall. Before long, we reach the Great Chamber, where Papa and Lady Anne are. There is a general hustle and bustle as the lords Papa has been meeting with move to leave, their discussions concluded. I spot the Earl of Northumberland, who I always think looks like a bear. James Metcalfe passes by me with Ralph Scrope of Upsall, and he ruffles my hair, grinning. I like James a lot. He lives nearby at Nappa and often visits. I wonder if he will stay around long enough for me to show him my new falcon, but at the moment, I hold back from asking. Some inner feeling tells me to, no matter how proud I am of my new possession.

I sidle into the room as they leave and stand by the window. As yet, no one notices me. Lady Anne talks to Papa quietly. Sir Robert Percy collects papers from a table. They look like maps, but he looks at Lord Lovell, and frowns. They have all been discussing the Scots. It looks like Papa may well be leaving home again soon.

"Frank, what have you there?" It is Sir Robert who speaks. He is a tall man, with thick black hair and merry eyes. Papa turns, only just seeing that his friend has entered the room. I back into a window embrasure, partially secluded by a thick arras. I do not want to leave.

Lord Lovell walks up to Papa slowly.

"Richard, this is from Hastings." Even from the tone of his voice I know there is something terribly wrong. Papa gives a half-smile, still holding a cup of wine in his hand, but Lady Anne has picked up on the tension. I see it in her face, the way her lips go thin.

"What does William want of me?" Papa asks. Sir Robert puts the maps back down on the table, watching.

"Dickon," Lord Lovell calls Papa by a name I know he only uses in private. My heart begins to beat very fast. "William begs you to go south with all due haste. Your brother, the king, is dead, God rest his soul." He pauses, for a moment. "God save King Edward."

The cup falls from Papa's hand and rolls around on the floor, spilling dark red wine like blood. The metallic sound makes me jump and Lady Anne turns around quickly. My hiding place is revealed but she only has time to give me a quick, disapproving glance, before she steps towards Lord Lovell, and takes the letter from his hand. As Papa stands rigidly still, as if in shock, Lady Anne reads the letter swiftly. Lord Lovell and Sir Robert exchange glances. They are worried, I can tell.

"He has been dead a week." Lady Anne says quietly and Papa finally moves, taking the letter from her hand, reading it slowly. His hand shakes, just a little. "My love," she whispers softly, "I would do anything to spare you this pain."

We all wait in silence. All I can hear is the crackling of the fire. Sir Robert clears his throat. Lord Lovell bites his bottom lip.

"My Lord, what does Hastings say of London?"

Papa folds the letter up and raises his head. His skin is pale. Lined. Why does he suddenly look so old?

"Edward died on the ninth day of April of a sudden fever. Hastings informs me that it is..." his voice stumbles for a second, but recovers, "...was - his last wish that I be named Lord Protector."

"That makes sense," remarks Sir Robert quietly. Lord Lovell purses his lips, seeming to consider.

"That may be, but not if you're Woodville I would imagine." Papa looks at Lord Lovell. There is a meaning in that look, but I do not know how to read the message there. He does, and looks down at the floor.

"Why would the queen herself not send a messenger? Surely she must have known that she needed to inform you of your brother's wishes?" Sir Robert's voice grows louder. I can see there is anger there. Lady Anne shoots him a grim smile as Papa answers.

"Hastings advises me to travel south with a large force. Elizabeth, deciding not to contact me directly, has instead summoned Anthony Rivers to bring young Edward back to London from Ludlow for his coronation." His eyes narrow, fix directly on his two friends. "Her intention is for him to enter London at the head of a large force. Hastings threatened to return to Calais if the Council approved this. He won the day. Edward will now travel with an escort of two thousand men only."

"Escort or army?" Sir Robert asks quickly. "Forgive me Richard, but is there any Vernage left? I sorely need something to wash this foul taste from my mouth!"

Lady Anne gives a small smile that does nothing to mask the worry in her eyes. She moves to a table and pours wine into silver goblets. Papa walks back into the centre of the room and throws the parchment on the settle. He folds his hands together, his thumb brushes swiftly across the rings on his finger.

"So," Lord Lovell says quietly, across the sound of wine being poured and to no-one in particular. "That's the way of it. She intends to ignore the will, and hopefully crown the Prince before you even get word of anything amiss. Hastings has been bold, thankfully."

Papa nods slowly, his head and eyes lowered, his fingers now toy with one of the rings on his left hand.

"I must go to London, that is not in dispute. How I go is another matter entirely." He considers his words for a moment. "I cannot be seen to be taking a northern force to the capital, with things being unsettled as they are. I do not even know if the issue of the Protectorship has been announced generally, or if Elizabeth is, as it would appear, rushing towards a coronation to avoid having to acknowledge the fact. She certainly has no intention of sending me word..." He pauses. "I can only then assume, as you say, that she intends to take a position as Queen Regent, in defiance of Edward's wishes."

Sir Robert takes an offered cup from Lady Anne's hand and drinks, swills the wine round in his mouth before he swallows.

"A Woodville Regency, with carefully placed family members in all of the noblest houses of the land. Would I be affording her too much credit if I believed she had almost foreseen this?"

I listen very carefully but do not really understand. King Edward is dead and his son will become king. His son, who is the same age as I am. My Mama told me how she shared sanctuary with the queen before I was born. How he is only a few months older than I am. That feels strange. How would I feel to be king?

I notice Lady Anne sigh. She hands a goblet of wine to Lord Lovell and stands before Papa, his goblet held against her chest, hands closed carefully around the stem. She fixes her gaze on Papa who has turned away from her slightly, so he will not see the worry in her eyes. Or her see his. I see it. I look at Lord Lovell. He sees it too.

"No Rob, I do feel she planned to build a power base from the very first. Don't forget, she was a Lancastrian widow, had previously lost her lands and status in a time of turmoil. She is far too scheming to allow that to happen to her a second time. Unfortunately, my brother was too immured by her charms to see it." He considers for a moment. "No, rather he did see it, and to a certain degree it amused him to accede to her. I doubt he ever expected to be dead by two score years." His voice trails off and once again he twists the ring on his smallest finger.

"How many?" Lord Lovell asks the question and I look up. How many what?

"Hmn?" Papa also seems puzzled by the question.

"How many men shall we take south?"

"No more than three hundred. We need to send word back to Hastings that we leave in two days. Rob, assemble the lords in the Great Hall, I will need to assess their intentions and affinity. I will travel to York first, where I will swear an oath of allegiance to our new king. From there we will go to meet the king's escort, so that as Lord Protector, I can accompany him into the capital and begin to plan the coronation. Once Edward is crowned..." Suddenly, it all becomes clear. Papa will now have to go to London to see the new king. My cousin, King Edward! Will we go too? Me, and Kathryn, and Edward?

I bite my lip. Edward has not been well. He fell into a fever just before my name day and is only just recovering. I cannot see that he will be allowed out of bed let alone on horseback.

Lady Anne has not moved from the sideboard where she still clutches the goblet of wine. Her eyes no longer hold worry, but glitter with what looks like anger. Lady Anne is rarely angry and once again I wonder at why this should be. Unless it is because it took so long for the message about the king's death to get here. After all, there are riders who travel the country in short order, making sure important messages get to their destination quickly. King Edward decreed it. Does it no longer happen now he is dead?

"Once Edward is crowned, she will announce herself Queen Regent and there will be no need for a Lord Protector." Lady Anne's voice is cold and her words shock me. I have never heard her speak this way before. "The boy has been closeted in Ludlow from the age of two, surrounded by her family, nurtured by Anthony, Lord Rivers. Do you really think you will make it as far as London? With only three hundred men to guard you against two thousand? Do you even think she will allow you to become Lord Protector after the boy is crowned? None of these people have any regard or respect for us, and now you think you can march into Westminster, after so many years away, and take control of a Woodville King? Good God, Dickon, apart from Hastings, I suspect, in fact, that there is more enmity than we know! Edward had great skill in dissembling to keep everyone either content or apart. I often thought there was more expediency than generosity in his awarding you so much tenure in the North! I refuse to allow us to pay the price for that man's lack of foresight!"

The air in the room fills with a stunned silence. Lord Lovell's eyebrows raise up to his hairline and I hear Sir Robert give a low exhaled whistle. The tension is broken by a bark of laughter from Papa, and he turns, also now noticing my presence. For a second he frowns, but then smiles at me. I smile back. He obviously thinks Lady Anne is silly. Everyone knows the queen is not Papa's enemy! She is King Edward's wife. Her children are our cousins, one of them was even named for Papa! I think of Kathryn. She often says silly things. She should stick to dresses and dancing. Everyone is smiling now.

"Anne, you have shocked our friends!" Papa crosses the room and takes the goblet from her hands. He turns to face us all, a grin curving into a smile. "You didn't know I wed a wildcat, did you?"

Sir Robert raises his goblet in Lady Anne's direction.

"Francis," he says cordially without looking in his friend's direction, his eyes firmly on Lady Anne, "remind me never to cross the Duchess of Gloucester!"

Everyone laughs, except for Lady Anne. But my father lifts her hand and kisses her fingers, and they both walk over to me, where I still stand by the wall, waiting.

"I didn't see you come in," Papa says gently. I look up at him, his eyes are a little hard behind the softness in his words. It makes me squirm just a little.

"I had been hawking with Lord Lovell. I was with him when the rider came."

He nods slowly.

"'Tis sad news, the death of King Edward." I have never seen him, but I know Papa loved him well. His eyes moisten with tears and I see Lady Anne's hand curl around his.

"It is." He agrees, and his voice sounds strange. As if something is caught up in his throat. "And as you have heard, now I must go to London."

"Will you go to his burial?"

Lady Anne shakes her head sadly. I see her fingers tighten.

"The King is already buried. At Windsor in a grand ceremony."

I know that will have hurt Papa very much. I look up at him, sadly.

"I am sorry Papa; I know he was your dearest brother. It is a shame we are so far away from London."

He reaches up then and strokes my hair. The touch is light, but strong. A strange mix.

"Thank you, John." I look from one to the other, waiting for a sign that I will find out what happens next, but they stand, looking at me.

"Will we go to London with you? Me, Kathryn and Edward?"

Lady Anne smiles, and lets go of Papa's hand. He moves away towards where Lord Lovell and Sir Robert stand talking quietly. She puts her arm around my shoulders, and turns me towards the door.

"No, John. There is no need for that. Your father will go to London and arrange the coronation. He will send a message for us to attend and after that we will return here. All it may mean is that your father has to visit

London more often. Until the king is of age."

Her grip on me feels oddly tight. But I am excited now that I will get to visit London. To dress in fine robes and be part of a coronation! Papa is an important man!

"May I go tell Edward?" I ask eagerly. "That we will be attending a coronation soon?"

She removes her arm and looks back into the room. The three men have their heads together, talking now in whispers.

"You may. He is much improved today, and would welcome a walk in the garden I think."

I suddenly feel very happy and excited. Edward is well again. And soon we will visit the great city of London together. I know we will have to put up with Kathryn and her airs and graces, but I don't care.

"I will take him to see my new falcon!" I tell her, and she smiles broadly.

"He will enjoy that very much."

I try to stop myself from hurtling over the covered bridge, nearly colliding with Papa's dog who grumbles at me as I thunder past, making for the round tower where Edward's chamber is. We are almost like noble princes ourselves! We will have fine clothes, and horses, and maybe Lir can come with me so I can hunt at Greenwich as Papa has told me about. Our new king is the same age as us, and it may be that we can all be friends! It will be a great adventure! I run into Edward's chamber, breathless, as he looks up, and laughs.

The Ribbon
December 1483

I love the holy season.

And this year it has been made much more special by the most precious gift which anyone could give. My brother was returned to me. He is much changed, that is true, and I hardly recognise him from the young boy who was taken from our family home and lodged with the Marquis of Dorset, the queen's brother.

We have both paid a price for our father's treason. But I think his is the greater. Yet it is not all bad. Now my uncle Richard sits on the throne, and who would have ever believed it possible? King Edward executed his brother and now his sons are declared illegitimate and can not aspire to their father's kingdom. Some would say that is divine justice.

I keep my own counsel.

But maybe now we can be happy. For even though my brother is still attainted, or else the throne would have been his and not uncle Richard's, we are together again. We have a place and status, and are treated well by the king and his queen, my aunt Anne.

"Lady Margaret?"

I look up into the face of the Lord Chamberlain, Francis Lovell. He is a quiet man, a kind man, with soulful brown eyes. He is the king's best friend, and very important.

"Lord Lovell." I meet his gaze. He is very handsome, particularly this evening, dressed in crimson velvet and blue silk. "Can I help you?"

He is smiling.

"I just wanted to express my thanks for your gift. Young Edward tells me it was your idea. I wanted you to know how very much it pleases me."

I look at the small, polished figure which he holds in his hand. It is a dog. A wolf-dog. Carved out of walnut.

"Lupellus," I say simply. "One of the symbols of your house. Edward has a rare gift. It pleases him to be able to make these small tokens."

He bows with the ease of a practised courtier and I smile.

"I am most touched."

As he moves on, I turn my eyes to my brother who is at the high table, a true honour for the son of a traitor, but my uncle never treats him so. He has made many gifts of carvings this year. A small boar for uncle Richard, a flowering rose for aunt Anne. A horse to be sent back to Middleham for our cousin Edward, who has not yet come to court. He also carved a Sun in Splendour for our cousin Bess, but she is still in sanctuary at the Abbey and I have no way of getting it to her. I will keep it for him until I can. If I ever can.

Edward loves to carve figures, mostly horses and knights, sometimes other animals. He draws battlefields and places the figures on them. He is happiest then. I do not know where he acquired this gift. I do not like to think of it. I think that he may have spent many hours alone, and found a way to pass the time. But, it keeps him content, and for that I am thankful.

It seems strange to see my aunt and uncle wear the crowns of kingship. I look around the room now. Many lords who attended King Edward's court are still here. The Stanley brothers, Suffolk, Northumberland. Then there is Norfolk, Lincoln, the Scropes of Bolton and Masham, and many other northern lords. But some who loved King Edward are no longer here.

There was a rebellion to put my cousins back on the throne. But they are gone now. I do not know where. Rumours have begun to seep through the palace walls and only today I heard one more. That they are dead. Smothered on my uncle's orders. But he would never do that. He would never harm children. No matter what their parents had, or had not, done. You only have to look around this hall to see that.

Also down from the north are my uncle's illegitimate children. His daughter Kathryn is dancing, her gown of burnished tawny silk billowing as she turns. Her hair gleams like polished copper, the candlelight catching the fire within. She is very pretty, and laughs a lot. She is laughing now. All the young squires are attracted to her, it is easy to see why.

Her brother John is over in the corner, talking to Sir James Tyrrell. John is dark, and looks like his father, how his father would have looked when he was younger I imagine. I like to look at John, but I have to glance away quickly if he sees me watching him. He is a little older, but I wish that he would notice me. But he will not. For I keep quiet, and remain in the background.

It was a skill I learned whilst at the court of Queen Elizabeth. After my father was executed, Edward was sent away to live with her son, the Marquis of Dorset, whilst I was left in the royal nursery. I was the same age as her son, Richard, who is also the Duke of York. And all his sisters were there too.

I knew my father had caused much trouble, and so I tried not to draw attention to myself. I tried to hide behind curtains and blend into walls. I feel I was successful; no one seems to pay much attention to me at all now. That is as it should be. As I wish it.

There is another who does not seek attention. I can see her, back there in the shadows. She does not dance. She eats at table and sometimes shares a word with Lord Lovell or Sir Robert Percy. Her name is Lady Desmond. She is truly beautiful and she is the mother of uncle Richard's illegitimate children, John and Kathryn.

She is Irish, and of noble blood. Tonight she is dressed in a simple green velvet gown, yet on her, it needs no adornment. I don't know why, but she seems to glow, even in the shadows. Her hair is the colour of fox-pelt and her eyes are as green as her dress. I have never spoken to her, I am not brave enough to do so. But she smiled at me once, and I wished that she had spoken to me. Or that I had been brave enough to speak to her.

It is getting late now, and the children are all leaving, ready for their beds. Edward runs towards me, his cheeks as pink as summer clover.

"Uncle Richard liked his boar! He said it was so real that he expected to hear it snort!" I smile and touch his hair. His hazel eyes are sparkling. I know he has my father's eyes as my aunt Anne told me. She said I favour my mother more. I don't remember much about either of them. It was all so long ago.

"Lord Lovell thanks you for his gift also," I tell him and he laughs.

"Did he say it barked?"

I shake my head and pick up our own gifts from the table. The king gave Edward a ring that belonged to our father. It is gold, and engraved with a bull's head. It is far too big for him and I will keep it for when he is grown. Maybe I will put it on a ribbon around my neck. I will keep it close. I hold my own gift of calf-skin riding gloves loosely in my hand. I have nothing of my mother's. Not a thing. She was a duchess and would surely have had jewels, books, maybe a mirror. But I do not know what happened to them.

"Come, it is time to go to bed now."

I lead him from the hall and we pass Lady Desmond and her children, unseen. They are all smiling. Lord Lovell and Lord Lincoln are with them. I hear Lady Desmond laugh. It is a pleasing sound. I am told that my uncle loved her. When he was younger. I wonder if he still loves her now?

We go up stairs to the private chambers but Edward suddenly stops in alarm.

"I forgot! I have a gift for you!"

I smile at him. I don't want to stop, not here. Too many people may pass by. I am still uncomfortable with people. I feel too many judge us for our birth. I feel they think we should not be here, at the king's court. Then, where should we be?

"Come, we must go."

He runs up the stairs two at a time and I have to hurry to keep up with him. Before long he is in the chamber which he shares with John, Lady Desmond's son. He fumbles under his pillow and comes back to stand before me. John's blue camlet cloak hangs on a peg and I long to go and touch it. To feel its softness under my hand, knowing he feels that too. It is a fancy and I shake my head.

"This is for you."

Edward hands me a black velvet pouch, tied with a ribbon. I open it and peer inside. I swallow, hard.

"Aunt Anne gave me the pouch. Do you like it?"

I clear my throat. For a moment I cannot speak.

"Did you show Aunt Anne what you had made?"

He grins widely. His small face is wreathed in pleasure.

"I did!"

"And what did she say?"

"She asked me if you would not prefer a flower or a kitten. But I told her that you had seen these in the courtyard. And you had stopped and touched them. So I knew you liked them. I knew you liked the shape!"

I managed a smile.

"It is lovely, Edward. Thank you."

He yawns then, the day catching up with him. When tiredness falls, it hits him with speed. I help him out of his best clothes and into his nightshirt and he climbs into bed. I lay beside him, my arm under his head, humming a tune I remember from somewhere, but I don't know where. I stroke his fair hair with my free hand and his head grows heavy after a short while, but I remain still as he sleeps.

The evening deepens and the noises in the palace begin to die down. The music stops, all becomes calm. I love this time of day. I love to roam the halls and passages alone, when I will not be seen. To think of where my father may once have walked. Where he and my mother may have shared a smile. A word. A kiss.

Eventually, I remove my arm from beneath Edward's sleeping form, and he opens his heavy lids.

"I love you, my sister," he mumbles, as if in a dream.

I place a kiss on his smooth, warm forehead.

"I love you too Edward. Go back to sleep."

He rolls over, pushing his thumb between his lips and my eyes fill with tears. But not for long. I have not cried in a long time. I cannot remember when.

John has not come to bed yet. I think he must be with Lady Desmond still. Perhaps she is keeping her children close tonight, sharing their memories of the day. I need to go before he arrives, even if I would really like to stay.

The palace is silent and I move down the passage, finding a secluded window seat. One lone torch flickers above my head and I sit. I empty the contents of the pouch into the palm of my hand. Then, I hear voices. Close, very close.

"I have had word from Burgundy. The boy thrives." It is my uncle's voice. A little weary. Uncertain.

"You did the right thing, Dickon, even though I know it still troubles you." Lord Lovell answers him. I hold my breath. I dare not move.

"I know. I would rather people think ill of me than put him where unscrupulous people would use him for their own ends. It is a pity Edward did not survive. Perhaps I should have…"

"Don't, Dickon! There was nothing else you could do. You had their best interests at heart. Just imagine if all of this had come out when George found out!"

George? My father George? Were they talking about my father?

"Maybe that would have been better. In the end." My uncle sounded very sad.

"Another rebellion? Another York rising? George played with fire Dickon. His knowledge could have set the country aflame."

"You could say I did that instead."

"No! You had no choice, Dickon. Edward had George executed because of what he knew. That should have been an end to it. No one expected Edward to die when he did. You had no choice. You had a moral and a legal duty. You are the rightful king. In time, this will all be forgotten. After a few years, you can bring Edward's son home."

There was a deep silence. How I was preventing myself from breathing, I will never know. Finally, my uncle spoke again.

"I always miss them this time of year. Edward. And George. He loved the festive season."

Lord Lovell chuckled softly.

"Of course he did. Edward always restocked the Malmsey!"

I heard a door close and the voices disappeared. Finally, I let out my breath, my mind spinning.

What was this? My cousin Edward was dead. How? When? His brother Richard was in Burgundy. Was he then with my aunt Margaret? I knew I had been right. I knew my uncle could never have harmed them. Even though they are illegitimate. As my uncle had found out once he came to London.

Their words still echoed in my head. But, how did my father fit into this? What did he do? What did he know that made his brother decide that he had to execute him to keep him quiet?

None of it makes much sense but I cannot stop thinking about it.

Slowly, I turn the wooden object around in my hand. It is a small, wooden barrel, grooved and polished. Just like the ones which the vintners delivered to the buttery the other day.

I heard tell that my father was drowned in a butt of malmsey. I had been looking at the size of it. Imagining what it would be like to be trapped in there.

Taking a deep breath, I clear my head.

I pull the black velvet ribbon from the pouch and thread it through the small, wooden carving, before tying it around my wrist.

It is late. Outside snow has begun to fall and I watch the flakes pile up against the window ledge and keep my own counsel.

The Rosary
October 1485

My father is dead.

My father is dead and another man sits on his throne.

My husband did very little as a Welsh exile from a bastard Lancastrian line marched across Wales. With an army made up of men spewed out of the pits of hell, he met my father in battle outside the city of Leicester. There, with the aid of the traitorous Stanley brothers and the covetous Earl of Northumberland, he killed my father. Well, not him. I hear he did not fight. That others fought for him whilst he sat and watched. Whilst he sat and watched my father charge towards him, courageously. The men of York recorded it so, as I hear it.

August sunlight glinting on his armour, glancing off the crescents of his crown. And afterwards...

How do I know? Not long after the battle, a soldier arrived at Raglan bearing Stanley livery. William was with his tenants, surveying the damage that the invading army had done to their crops. Many will go hungry this winter. The man had bright blue eyes, and sounded a little like my mother. He handed me a small leather pouch and a letter, addressed to me in a hand I did not recognise, not immediately. Then he left, quickly. Riding away on a bay courser at great speed.

So many I remember are dead. Sir Richard Ratcliffe, who I was always a little frightened of. He was so sombre. Sir Robert Brackenbury. Gentle Sir Robert, who always had a kind word for me and my brother John. Then there was another John. John Kendall, my father's secretary, working tirelessly through the hours at my father's elbow. Sir Robert Percy... I miss his smile already.

I cannot believe I will never see them again. Never hear my father's voice again. I miss my mother so! She will need me. She will be inconsolable with grief and I want to go to her. William tells me I have to wait. That we will go to London to pay allegiance to the king. The king who killed my father. How can I do that? How can I watch him take my father's place? Bear Lord Stanley's self-satisfied smirk? His wife's grating self-righteousness? How can I do that and not scream?

I am big with my husband's child, and should soon be entering my confinement. But instead, we go to London. I do not want to go but we have no choice. Our loyalty is in question and the new... I cannot say it. Not yet. He demands we pledge our loyalty. No matter that our child protests at the journey almost every mile along the road. William will not hear my worries. He tells me that my cousin John, the Earl of Lincoln, who was also my father's heir, has bent the knee. I try not to see his handsome face, as it still pierces my heart, for once I thought I loved him. And not so long ago, but it was not to be. So why does it still hurt so, that he could so easily forget his king? Forget me?

But what of my brother, I ask him, only to have him shake his head. There has been no news of him, my mother or my cousins Edward and Margaret. Only news of Bess, the eldest of the York princesses. She will marry her uncle's murderer. The thought makes me feel sick.

William is talking again now. Of Lord Lovell. He has been attainted and lost all his lands and titles. At first they thought he was dead, slaughtered on the field of battle. But I knew differently. I can feel the stiff parchment of his letter close to my skin. How or when he managed to write it I know not, but I knew that were he alive he would let me know. I can see him sitting on the grass next to me, strumming his lute under a summer sky on the banks of the River Cover. He has a cleft in his chin, as if someone pressed their thumb there when he was being formed. He told me a story that day, of a falcon he once owned which would not hunt. Of how he made a gift of it to his wife. Anna.

I can still see her, that first day I met her at Middleham. So young and shy I thought she was Lord Lovell's sister. She did not stay at Middleham long, and I thought Lord Lovell may be sad after she had left and would often try to make him smile. He is my father's most beloved friend, and my father is dead.

I remember one Christmas, when the snow lay deep and soft against the tall grey walls. It was the winter of my fourteenth year, and Lord Lovell took me by the hand and led me in the Basse Dance, and I felt the grandest lady in the land. I had on my best gown of damson velvet, trimmed with gold brocade and he treated me in such a courtly manner that I think I fell a little in love with him that night, as he walked beside me, his hand resting behind him, placed lightly on the base of his spine. My father sat at the high table with Lady Anne, both of them beaming happily, my half-brother Edward at their side, admiring the new jewelled dagger that had been a gift from our father.

At the end of the dance, Lord Lovell had twirled me right merrily under the mistletoe, and kissed me on my cheek and told my I grew more like my mother every day. Then he grew very sad, and kissing my fingers, he left me and walked over to the high table to speak to my father. I think he was missing Anna, for she was not there that night. He always seemed to be there when I needed someone to talk to, when we were both at Middleham. It seems such a long time ago now. I wonder where he is now and pray that he is well.

We pass Newgate and enter the city at Ludgate. So, we are not to go to Westminster directly. The babe is restless in my belly and my feet hurt, they feel too large for my boots and I long to kick them off. We pass the Blackfriars and St Paul's, and it is only when I see the massive gatehouse of

Baynard's Castle rise before me that my heart lightens. I was only young when I lived there, but I have memories of sunlight, music and my mother's laughter. I wonder if I will be allowed to see her, and my heart begins to race.

There are red dragon banners flying above my grandmother's former home and I wonder what this means. I don't know where she is now. There is so much I don't know. Some surly men watch us dismount and I clutch on to Will's hand as he leads me into the castle, and for a moment I feel a little dizzy. Something feels wrong, but I do not know what it is.

Something just feels very wrong.

Will's face creases in concern and he leads me to the window seat in the solar. I do not let go of his hand until I can rest back against the faded, embroidered cushions. Strangely, I remember each silken petal, each twisting vine. It is like coming home and I try to relax, try to breathe deeply, calming the anxiety which is fighting to overwhelm me.

"My lord?"

A voice calls for Will's attention, but he does not immediately turn. He is looking at me, carefully. I smile to try and melt away his worry. We do not love each other, that much we both know. But he is kind and affectionate, and did not seem to know that my heart lie with another. It is strange, I think, that in this way I am also so much like my mother. That we were both bastard born. That we both loved a man with royal blood who married another. Yet, father is dead, and I hope that I do not see my cousin John, standing at Henry Tudor's side.

"My lord?" The servant is insistent, and Will turns away from me. I look out of the window at the river, today it is blue and sparkling. A gaily coloured barge forges its way downstream, no doubt bound for Westminster. Where we shall shortly be summoned. I close my eyes and rest my head back and let the sun warm me. I could stay here forever. It is so peaceful and quiet and I never did feel at home in Wales.

A distant bell tolls, waking me from a half-slumber. How long have my eyes been closed? A minute? An hour? Will is standing before me, his face a mask of grim concern. He is biting his lip.

"You look very pale."

"I am fine. The journey wearied me a little. That is all." It is true. I do feel better than I did. Just a little. I just so wish to take off my boots as my ankles are beginning to throb. I can feel my heartbeat in them. This does nothing to change his expression. His eyes are troubled. Will never was a man for merriment. He looks down at his hands. At the letter there.

"We are to attend the king tomorrow morning. At Westminster."

I nod, averting my eyes. At least I can rest overnight. Can recover before I look into the eyes of the man who was responsible for my father's death. For what was done to him afterwards. Who denied him even the most basic dignity. Even common people receive more in death than he did, and he was an anointed king. He was my father.

Tears sting my eyes but I fight them back and smile. I am the daughter of a king.

"I will retire to a chamber if I may?" I say, looking up at him. "I would like to be well rested." A thought occurs to me and I look around. "Will I return to Wales for my confinement do you think? Or will it be here?" This pleases me as my mother spent her confinement here, before I was born.

Will swallows hard and folds the letter back together. He looks uneasy now, as we talk about our child, and it is then I realise I am a fool. My child will have the blood of the Plantagenet family. Of the House of York. As do I. Was the timing of our journey truly a coincidence? Will clears his throat.

"There is something else."

I think my heart would lurch to the pit of my stomach had the babe not been in the way. I say nothing. I wait. My hands grip the careworn fabric either side of my skirts.

"Your brother John has been consigned to the Tower."

"I know this," I reply steadily. "My mother has been given an apartment there."

There is a deadly pause.

"He was. He is now imprisoned there. He is in a tower cell."

There it is. The bell which tolled is now echoed in my heartbeats. If there was ever a bell at all.

"My cousin of Warwick. Is he still housed in the Tower?"

His fair brows knot together.

"How did you know that?"

How did I know? I cannot tell him.

"Servants' gossip. Bad news is fleet of foot."

I do not understand why, but I am strangely calm. As if I once read of all this in the pages of a book, and am familiar with how the tale will end. I push myself up from the window seat, and he reaches out to help me. I take his hand.

"Do you not want to know what he did?"

Carefully, I traverse the two steps down from the window. The air around me seems very light, almost translucent. I look up into Will's eyes once more. I cannot read what is behind them. Or I do not want to.

"I know why. And so do you." He colours rapidly. At least he has the decency to look embarrassed. "I will go to chapel and pray for his safekeeping, if you will excuse me?"

He nods, and I pick up my skirts, following the path across the solar which I had so often seen the Duchess Cecily take. I hardly reach the door when he speaks.

"Kathryn?"

I halt. But I do not turn around.

"I am sorry."

His words are a buzzing in my ears. Like an insect, and I am glad when I can no longer hear them. It is not his fault he is a Welshman, and so is the usurper Tudor. Not his fault at all. Yet at this moment I cannot bear it and the two become one in my mind. My steps quicken as I pass through the doorway and down the passages, until I reach the solitude of the chapel. The sun has disappeared behind a cloud and the stained glass images are darkly dour. I can smell incense, and it has with it a hint of violet. My mother's fragrance.

I am clumsy, but I get down on my knees before the altar, my eyes fixed on the crucifix as I cross my breast with my hands. Slowly, my fingers steal into my pocket and find the rosary there. I kiss the small, golden cross, the sapphire beads warm in my hands. Words swim before my eyes, drowning in my tears. Yet I can see them clearly.

"My dearest Kathryn. I hope this reaches you and that you are well. Disaster has befallen us as you now know. I have word that both your mother and brother are safe, and are being given care as affords their station, but that your cousin Warwick is already locked away in a tower cell. Before he sent me to the south, your father gave me the rosary which I have asked Conor to place in your hand. Do not be alarmed by his livery. His heart is true. The rosary belonged to Duchess Cecily and she gave it to your father as he travelled to Nottingham before battle was joined. As I knew him, I know he would have held this most precious to his heart, and so I was both honoured and overwhelmed when he gave it to me for my safety during the events to come. I cannot return it to him, much to my despair, so I return it to you, the daughter he loved so well. When you see your mother, tell her I will not desist from my efforts to restore the House of York. Tell her that as I loved your father, my love for her will spur me on through the times to come. For yourself, know that I love you as the daughter I never had. A love that grew with each step you took and each word you spoke. Do whatever you must to keep yourself safe, it is what your father would have demanded from you. I hope one day to see you again, God willing, and may Our Lady have mercy on us all during these troubled times. Your heartily loving friend, Francis Lovell."

Does he mean he loved my mother, truly? Or, does he speak of an affection that matched his undoubted devotion to his king? His friend? I want to ask him, more than anything. I want to see him. See his face warm with a smile, see my mother's eyes when she looks at me. I want... I want...

I sense someone is standing behind me, and I try to turn, but pain rips through my body, making me gasp. Sweat drenches me, and the room begins to whirl. The sun comes out, the window now a skein of colour, the skirts of one hundred ladies dancing at a Christmas court. Another wave hits me, pain like sharpened knives plunging into my belly, and I cry out.

"Papa!"

I turn, knowing to do so will almost tear me in two, but from somewhere I summon up the strength, cradling my belly in my arm. I can see him, he is there! I know it is him! He is wearing his dark blue riding cloak, his crimson robe, and his hand is outstretched towards me. I begin to sob wildly. I did not know the pain would be like this.

"Kathryn." I look up at him. His eyes are a summer storm. His face full of familiar care. "Daughter, take my hand."

I reach out, pain coursing through every fibre of my being, but I place my hand in his, curl my fingers around, feel the familiar jewels he wears. The rosary falls to the floor, but I cannot pick it up. I hear it fall, but I cannot see it.

It doesn't matter.

My father is here and all will be well.

The Innocent
1487

It's black. Dark.

It's been dark a long time - but it's not cold anymore. Does that mean it is summer? You would think it would be lighter - if it was summer. You would think I would know, but I only sense it. Somehow. I can't see my feet, but I know they are bare. I can still feel every crack and crevice in the rough, stone floor. Even that doesn't seem as cold as it was. It must be summer then?

Summer. The sky – an impossible forget-me-not blue. Clouds racing each other across the hills like horses - leaving shadow prints on the fields. Green as new willow buds, shyly unfurling. Green, dark and sumptuous like my sister's best velvet gown, rippling as she twirled joyfully in the dance. Green. My mother's eyes - lustrous with tears. Like jewels.

I miss birdsong - more than anything - which is strange. I try to remember the warble of a blackbird at dusk, full throated - as it bids good night to the sun setting in a lavender gauze sky.

I stood there once, and saw and heard. High up on the battlement, as night fell all around me, wrapping me in the balmiest of breezes. It covered me like a cloak, warm and sumptuous. Stars opening their winsome eyes one by one. A crescent moon, shaped like a scythe, hung brightly in the sky. My father lay his hand on my shoulder - and all was well as torches flared into life below us. One by one. Like fireflies!

I can see it all, even now. Even though it has been dark for as long as I can remember.

Even when the door opens, I do not see light. When my bread and ale appear as if conjured by a spirit, I smell its presence more than I see it. Enough to scrabble down and find the hard, stale knob of cocket. Stale. Where once I had my pick of the finest demain bread, served on a platter. My teeth are getting sore now, and it hurts to eat. But I swallow it down - grateful. But my mouth is already so dry.

I find the cup. Drink. It's foul tasting, but soothes my ragged throat. Sometimes, I think the guards have mixed in other things too unspeakable to think of. Sometimes I can smell it. But I drink it anyway. There is nothing else.

Summer. If it is - I have been here many months. More than half a year. It was cold then, when they brought me here. Yet, if it is summer now...no! I cannot think of it - for it then was two years ago since I kissed my father's cheek and watched him leave. He was smiling - and did not smile often then. I wanted to cry, I was afraid. But my mother was watching, and her fingers almost crushed the bones of my hand to dust.

It was the last time I saw him. Riding, bare-headed, in the early morning sun, his midnight cloak swathing Surrey's muscular flanks. I could swear a lark was singing a plaintive farewell. I miss birdsong.

And my mother' voice.

It has a velvet lilt. Once, she would rock me close to her chest, softly singing words I didn't understand. I was her 'mhuirnín' - her 'a'stor' and her embrace was soft as goose down, fragrant as flowers. Violets. Royal purple - pricked with saffron. My throat stings with unshed tears.

Mama? Are you safe? I pray to our lady I will see you again, but that I will be dressed in the finest camlet, with silken hose. Crimson I think. The colour of the jewel you wear on your finger. So often I saw you caress it with your thumb, staring into the firelight, lost in thought, your hair putting the flames to shame. Sometimes I know you wept, yet softly, and not for long. You didn't want me to see, so I didn't.

I wouldn't want you to see me here. It is dark - but I know how I look. I can smell how bad I am. From what I must do in this filthy hole. I couldn't bear to see you weep for me. Not for me. Not your brave boy.

I will be brave. Like father was. The bravest prince in all the land. The bravest king. Do the bravest always die? And the cowards win?

The new king is a coward. He lies about why he keeps me here. He says I wrote to my mother's' family in Ireland - but I didn't. It is not true. Like so many things being said now. I am here because he is a coward. He hides me here because I am a York prince. He's frightened of a boy. A bastard boy.

No. Mama told me that is no slur. Noble blood runs beneath my skin. Irish earls and English kings - has that Welshman so proud a lineage?

Wales. My sister is in Wales. Mama told me she was to have a child. I hope she is safe and stays far away from London. It is a dangerous place now. Cold and treacherous. Dank. Full of sickness. I am safer down here. Maybe, then, I should not mind so much.

I have never been sick. Not really. Not that I can remember. I fell off my horse a few times and hit my head once. That was the worst. He was called Lance, my horse. After Lancelot. In the tales of Arthur. One day, my brother Edward begged to ride him. Well, not my brother, exactly. We had the same father, but Edward's mother was the Lady Anne. Then, for a while, the queen. Slim, pale and very pretty. Like a flower. She loved him very much, but he was too often ill. Poor Edward.

He tried so hard to be like me, I think. Following me everywhere. From those first days we played in the sun-filled bailey, I knew we would be friends. He was younger than me, but that didn't matter. And when he rode Lance, I shouldn't have let him, but I could refuse him nothing. He had not been well, but I helped him mount and soon he was cantering around in the sunshine.

Sunshine.

There were birds singing, their jubilant notes drifting over the high, grey walls. Then, suddenly, Edward fell forwards, folded up like one of those straw filled sacks we used at the quintain. He began to slide from the saddle, and I could not move. Like I can't move much now, but different. I thought he would hit the ground and surely die. I had never been so frightened. Not then. I have been frightened since. Since last summer.

But my Lord Lovell had seen him and ran like the wind, catching Edward in his strong arms before he could come to harm. He gave me a hard, reproving look, but said nothing else, and before Lady Anne could find out, Edward was back in his chamber. No-one found out. Lord Lovell kept it secret. I would never have brought him harm, my brother Edward. I was not there when he died, when he tried so hard to live.

Edward kept the secret too, and repaid me in kind. One day I watched in envy as Papa allowed him to ride his magnificent destrier, White Surrey, the most magnificent beast I had ever seen. An animal fit to bear the knights of King Arthur. Papa walked Edward around the bailey and we all watched. Lady Anne stood beside me, wringing her hands in fear. I think she would have stopped it if she could.

Then, as I went to turn away, Edward said something to Papa. I know he did, and suddenly, he called out my name, and I was allowed to ride. Papa even acted as my squire, helping me to mount White Surrey without a mounting block. I rode like the wind that day, and people cheered and smiled. Lord Lovell applauded the loudest, I think, and slapped me on the back when I dismounted. I have ridden many horses since that day. But none like White Surrey. He also died bravely I heard.

Lord Lovell was a good man. Some say he is dead too. So many men are dead now. Will I be dead soon, before I am even really a man?

I don't want to die.

If the Tudor king wants me to, I will go far away, and take my mother and my sister with me. We will be no trouble. We mean no harm to him, even after what he did to my father. Even though at first, yes, I wanted to kill him. When I heard what he had done. What he allowed to be done. I can't think of it. Not while I am in here. Not ever. I fear the thought of it may drive me mad. If I begin to think of it, I fear I will not be able to stop.

My cousin of Lincoln has forgiven him. Tudor. I cannot go that far. I could not serve him, not even if he commanded me to. Not to see him in my father's place day after day. At least down here I do not have to see him. In his chair. In his crown. Eating at the high table from the same silverware, below the cloth of state. To greet him by a royal name. No. This darkness is better than that.

I am weary but do not sleep. I don't think I do. It is hard to tell the difference between the dark and sleep. One runs endlessly into the other –

like a river into the sea. It is hard to tell if my eyes are closed or open. It is all much the same. Only if I dream, do I know I am truly asleep. And dreams are few, thankfully, for they only tantalise me with what used to be. Of what should be, if it were not for him. For Tudor. Am I dreaming now, for I can hear sounds? Noises. Feet. Almost like marching.

It is usually so quiet; it is like a rolling thunder. Has someone attacked the Tower? I heard talk of rebels before they threw me down here. God save us! Have the men of the north come to wreak vengeance for my father? For the king they professed to love? My heart is racing. My chest hurts. I can feel my own breath hot on my face.

I hear the door to my chamber crash open and there are voices. Gruff, too loud. Someone is laughing raucously. It claws at my ears.

Suddenly, strong hands grip my arms, and I am pulled to my feet. But I fall again, my knees almost breaking against the hard stone of the floor. A man cackles. I feel blood trickling down my shins as they make me stand again. It is a long time since I stood. My legs struggle to bear my weight, such as it is now.

"Bastard whelp!" someone growls, and I am pulled along, held up by the armpits, fingers digging in my flesh, my toes grazing along stone. I cannot resist. They are tall and strong. I am too weak. Strange. I was never weak.

Stairs, now. I am being dragged up some stairs and there is more laughter, low and cruel. I hear a voice whisper by my ear.

"Are you crouchback like him? Spawn of the devil that you are? We'll find out soon enough lad, don't you worry!"

I try to swallow and nearly choke, my mouth coated with sand. I cannot speak, even if I wanted to. Even if I wanted to defend the truth. What good is it now? Who would hear me other than these low, base men.

"Bloody murdering bastard, he was!" Another voice, cold and dispassionate. "Well, 'tis Fortune's Wheel. It comes around and goes around. 'Tis true justice we do today, and that be a fact. As old King Edward lost his two sons, so will Old Dick."

For a minute I do want to speak, to ask them what they mean, but then, before I can, the dark explodes into a nimbus of light so bright I want to scream. The hood that has blinded me for so long is ripped off my head and I screw up my eyes, try to make them water. But there is no liquid left in my body. I have cried more than I have drunk in.

They keep me standing. Just. It is silent. Silent as the grave. My eyes begin to make out shapes, colours. Slowly. I see the crenellations of the wall with a cornflower-blue sky above, clouds. There they are, as I remember them, racing like horses. It is beautiful.

A banner snaps in the breeze, I can hear it. My ears can somehow hear everything. I can hear the river, flowing beside the walls, the clank of chains against the embankment stone, boats moving along in the water. I can't stop looking upwards, straining my neck for fear the vision will disappear as suddenly as it appeared.

Faces now, around me. Four men. They wear scarlet clothes. Like blood. They are robed in the colour of murder. I don't know them but each one wears a satisfied grin. Apart from one man, who pushes me forwards roughly. I stumble, almost fall. I see my feet, dirty, bruised, my toes bloody, and I look back up.

I wish I hadn't looked up. There's a block there. I have seen them enough to know what it is. What is it for? There is no one else here. Just these men.

Am I to die then? Dear Father, am I to die now? I am frightened. I can smell the fear on my skin. Can they? Will they see how scared I am and tell the Tudor king that I died in fear? That I was not my father's son? That at the very end I was a craven coward?

"My son?"

I look around, blinking. For a second, I thought it was my father speaking to me, so gentle were the words. Yet, it is a priest. His face is old, lined with age, and kindly. He hands me a rosary. Beads of amber and jade. My mother's face swims before my eyes and I fall to my knees for his blessing, ignoring the pain. There is no pain. There is only the quiet, the soft whisper of the priest's benediction as he asks the lord to absolve me of my sins.

I know the sky is still blue even though my eyes are closed now, but I will not weep. Calm descends, every other emotion floods away. I am thankful. I can feel the Grace of God, for he knows I am innocent of whatever callow men choose to accuse me of. I know I will soon see my father; his storm-grey eyes will smile at me. I will hear him laugh now that he has shed the cares of this world. And the Lady Anne, with her soft voice and delicate hands. Edward. Free of worldly pain. They will be my family, as they always have been.

I whisper the pater-noster, the borrowed beads cool in my fingers. I am finally free. Free of the dark.

It is summer. I knew it was. I hear the song of the lark, soaring free and wild, somewhere high up in the sky.

I smile.

I have missed the birdsong.

The Lamb
April 1484

There is a patch of blue sky I can see through my window. Now and again a single cloud roams across the sky and I watch it move slowly until is disappears behind the wall of my chamber, changing as it goes. Sometimes, they make shapes. I thought I saw a boar, and one day a crown. But Mistress Idley thinks I am fanciful. I can see it from the look on her face.

I wanted to sit at the window and look down across the village, but I feel too weak today. I did not sleep well last night. I kept waking up a lot. Sometimes because I was very hot, or because my belly griped and I needed to go to the gardrobe. So Mistress Idley tells me to stay abed today.

I am pleased to, although I did not admit it. My legs feel heavy. I am sure I will feel better after a bit more rest. I might protest more if John was here. Or Kathryn. They are my brother and sister, but they have a different Mama. She came here once. The Lady Desmond, her name is. She is very pretty and comes from Ireland. All green and gold! Like sunset through autumn leaves, if you stand by the river as the sky turns red.

Kathryn looks like her Mama. I do miss her very much. She has a pet name for me. She calls me her 'Lamb.'

It was a jest at first. I had been ill and was very wobbly on my legs when I finally got up from my bed. She laughed and said I was like a spring lamb in the field. But I know she was not being cruel. The next time I had a fever, she sat by my bedside, and stroked my head with a cool, damp cloth. She sang to me, songs I did not understand, but which soothed me none the less. Songs she said her Mama sung to her. Before she went to bed, she would kiss my forehead and whisper, "Sleep well, my little lamb."

Now I have just Mistress Idley. She fusses too much, but has cared for me for a long time. Alice, my other nurse, went back to Pontefract, that was when my father sent for Mama. She had to go and join him in London, when he became king. John and Kathryn went too. They all saw Mama and Papa crowned, which must have been a grand affair.

But I could not go. Kathryn wrote and told me how splendid they looked, and how everyone cheered and the streets were hung with tapestries and banners! There were bells ringing, musicians and wine flowed from the fountains! It made me very sad that I could not be there to see all of that. To see how the people of London loved my Papa.

I thought it would not be too long before I would join them, but it will not be long now, I think.

I have to be well first, so that I do not worry Mama and Papa. In summer, I hope. I cannot wait to visit vast cities like London and Nottingham. I would very much like to see the sea. Mama has promised me I will. And now it will be my duty to visit Wales too!

For last year, I went to York and was made Prince of Wales, in the palace by the magnificent Minster Church. There were many important people there, although I cannot remember their names. Apart from the Dean, Robert Booth. He looked very stern, as sometimes holy men do. It must be serious business, I think, looking after souls and carrying out the will of God.

I wore a heavy robe made of cloth of gold. Papa put a cap on my head, and placed a shiny, gold ring on my finger. Then he girded a sword around my waist, kneeling down before me, and he looked so very happy. I cannot remember him ever looking quite so happy. He called me 'our dearest firstborn son, Edward' and Mama was crying. The candlelight made her tears sparkle like stars.

Papa then put a golden staff in my hand and walked before me bearing a grand sword of state. It was too large for me to carry even though it was made especially for the Princes of England. And I am one now. I will inherit Papa's throne one day and will sit on the King's Bench in Westminster Hall.

John was made a knight in York, and so was my cousin Edward of Warwick. I had not met him before. He was very quiet, and said little. Not like John who was so excited he could hardly stop talking all evening.

Kathryn was very fair. Her dress was crimson and gold and she had pearls in her hair. Not long after that she was married, to the Earl of Huntington. My sister Kathryn – a Countess! She lives in Wales too now and so I will be able to visit with her when I go. It must truly be a wonderful place!

Her Mama was in York too and they looked so alike! Lady Desmond spent a lot of time with Lord Lovell. She made him laugh a lot. I never saw him laugh that much when he was here. He always seemed so serious. But then, Papa kept him very busy. As he does now. He is the King's Chamberlain. A very important man. The most important man at Papa's court! I will have John as my Chamberlain, for Papa said Lord Lovell is his very best friend, and that is why he was chosen. And that is why I will choose John, when my turn comes.

When I close my eyes I can still see all the rich clothes, the silk and jewels, shimmering in the golden light. The altar at the Minster had figures on it. The twelve Apostles in gold and silver. They looked as grand as the congregation that day! It was like a dream and I look at the gold band which still sits on my finger. I have never taken it off. It was not a dream. I will be king one day!

The door creaks and Mistress Idley comes in. She peers at me with narrowed eyes.

"Have you been sleeping?" I shake my head. I do feel weak, but not tired. She walks over to my bed and bends over, looking at me more closely.

"Well, I have something for you, but I don't want you getting over excited."

She places her cool hand on my forehead, frowns a little. I push myself up against the pillows, brushing her fingers away.

"What is it? Is it from Papa?"

Papa is in Nottingham. There is a big castle there built on a rock. He tells me you can see for miles and miles around, all around the kingdom! I cannot wait to see it myself.

Mistress Idley holds out a letter. I knew it was a letter!

"It is from Wales." She smiles. Her face creases up, making her eyes small and shiny and her cheeks puff out.

"Kathryn!" I reach out eagerly. It is a while since I heard from her and my heart beats a little quickly.

She nods happily and I take the letter from her hand.

"You read it and I will go fetch you some broth. I would like to see some colour in those cheeks before night falls!" She bustles out, pleased with herself.

I would protest. I am not hungry but I want her to go so I can read the letter, so I do not say anything. The door closes and I crack the seal. It has a lion on it. I swallow hard. I often forget, she is a married lady now. The parchment crackles in my hand.

"My dearest Lamb, I hope this letter finds you well. Papa tells me you have been ailing again, but I know you will not fail for long and soon you will be fit and strong and will come down from the north. He also tells me you are to go to Nottingham soon, to meet him there. I am sad that I will not be able to see you as I am now at my new home in Wales. A grand, married lady! Just like Lady Anne! I have horses, cooks and servants. I have a lady-in-waiting and she follows me around like one of Papa's hounds! She even looks a little like one! I hope John has written to you too, I asked him to. He is still training to be a great knight and says he wants to cross the sea one day. To France. Or to Ireland to see Mama's home. Write to me when you are at Nottingham, and ask Papa if you can come to court for the Holy season. We can dance and play tricks, just like the Lord of Misrule! I cannot wait to see you again and for us all to be together. Written at Raglan, the twentieth day of February, your heartily loving sister, K."

I lay back against my pillows and look back out of the window. I try to imagine Kathryn as lady of the castle. Welcoming lords and ladies to supper, ordering servants about and helping with the accounts, as Mama sometimes does with Sir John. It makes me smile. In my mind, she is always without her shoes.

As soon as she would come in here to visit me, she would always take off her shoes, throwing them across the room. John used to chide her and tell her she was like one of the peasant children, running around in the mud with dirt between her toes. But he was wrong. Her feet were always clean. Maybe dusty sometimes, but clean. I know because she would stretch out her legs and wiggle her toes to show me. It always made me laugh.

Mistress Idley comes back with a pewter bowl, full of steaming broth. I can smell it. It smells of capon, and she has a wedge of freshly made bread. I know I will have to try and eat some of it, but I am still not hungry.

Determined, she sits down in the chair beside the bed.

"How is the Countess?"

My eyebrows raise. It always surprises me. My sister has a grand title.

"She has servants." I say simply. I want to keep the letter to myself. Mistress Idley smiles, stirring the broth busily.

"That sounds very grand." She passes the bowl over to me and I take it from her, eyeing it with caution. I hope there is not much in there, as I do not feel I can eat a lot. But, obediently, I dip in the spoon and drink some of the hot liquid. It tastes of very little. Maybe the bread will taste better. I look at it, unconvinced. She is watching me, closely. I swallow and lick my lips.

"When will I be able to go to Nottingham? To see Mama and Papa?" He said I could go. He said he would be there in April, and it is April now."

She brushes her skirts with her hand, as if she sees something there that I do not.

"You have to get well first. So that you can make the journey."

I take another spoonful of the watery liquid.

"I am well. Just a bit weak still. But I could go in a litter, could I not?"

She smiles at me kindly; one blue-veined hand pats the counterpane.

"Now, don't you think it would be better to wait until you could ride there? Think how proud His Grace would be to see you trot up to the castle, all booted and spurred like the young prince you are!"

I know she is right, but I want to see them so much it hurts. I don't mind if I have to travel in a litter. It could be more than a week before I feel strong enough to make a journey to Nottingham on horseback. And... What if the fever comes back before then? What if I began shaking again? Why can I not go now, tomorrow, before anything else prevents it?

It will be too late once I am at Nottingham Castle. If I get ill there, at least Mama and Papa can tend to me. The thought of this makes me attack the broth with more enthusiasm. Perhaps Mistress Idley will change her mind if she sees me eat more. If she sees I am really getting well.

As she watches, I eat every last drop of broth and follow with the bread. Every last morsel. It makes me feel too full and a little sick, but I hand the bowl back with a grin.

"Good lad!" I bask in her approval. "Carry on like that and you will soon be cantering down to Tanfield and beyond!"

The food lies heavy in my stomach, but it is worth it to hear those words. Perhaps I ate too quick, but I swallow and smile. I want to read my letter again, but my eyelids feel suddenly heavy.

"I think I will sleep now. Just a while." Mistress Idley nods, she cradles the empty bowl in her hands.

"Very well. Would you like me to read to you?" I shake my head. All I want to do now is sleep. She touches my hair gently as I sink down into my pillows and I hear her leave the room.

I hear other sounds as I drift down into a soft darkness. I can hear the smithy, the beat of his hammer against the anvil, like a bell. Horses neigh and whinny, loudly, as if they stand below my window. I hear people talking, murmured conversations. Laughter. One of the dogs bark. I even think I can hear Sir John. He talks about getting the litter ready for my journey. I think I am smiling as I fall asleep.

Then, I am riding! Cantering wildly over the plain towards William's Hill! Kathryn is beating me though! She rides ahead of me, her red cloak billowing out behind her like a banner, her long auburn hair streaming out like flame! She laughs and laughs.

"Catch me, Edward! Come on! You can catch me!"

She looks back and I see the mischief in her eyes. Eyes as green as oak leaves. She spurs her bay on harder and I take the challenge.

Digging in my heels, I begin to close on her. The wind is in my hair too, rushing past my ears. It sounds like the river! I have never ridden so fast! It makes me breathless but feels so wonderful. My legs are strong, gripping tightly to my lyard. My horse is silver-grey, like White Surrey, but his name is Lux. Blanc Lux. White Light. And today he flies like the wind!

Kathryn reaches the hill first and dismounts, laughing, her skirts askew in a most unladylike manner. She does not care. Her face is flushed, and as always she looks so pretty. I ride up to her, but she is already climbing up the hill, skirts caught up in her hands, her feet bare, moist with dew.

I slide from my saddle, afraid that I will not be able to keep up with her but I can! My legs are strong, and I can feel my heart racing. I bound up to the top of the hill without effort, where she is waiting for me, her face wreathed in smiles. She throws her arms around me as I breach the top. She smells of sunlight and roses, and we throw ourselves onto the ground, pausing to catch our breath.

"The sky is so close!" Kathyrn breathes merrily. "We could be in heaven!"

I sit with my knees clasped to my chest. From up here we can see back down to the castle, see the banners unfurling and snapping in the breeze. The river Cover winds its way across a tapestry of green, like a silken ribbon. The air is balmy. Fragrant. Kathryn still lies on her back looking at the clouds. I watch her. Her arms lay above her head, pillowed in the cloak of her hair. Her chest rises and falls as her breathing returns to normal.

I cannot believe I have such a wondrous creature for a sister. I wish she would be with me always. I wish I could feel like this forever. I am not tired or weak. I feel I could run for miles and miles. I could hurtle down the side of the hill and not stop until I reach the river, plunging myself in to feel its coolness wash over me like summer rain.

"This used to be a castle," I say simply. She turns her head to look at me.

"Perhaps it still is. Our castle! You are king and I am queen!" That makes me laugh.

"You are my sister, silly. You cannot be my queen!" Although, I wish she spoke the truth. She pouts prettily and sits up, her hair falling down over her shoulders, shining like silk.

"Then Lambs cannot be a king!" She sighs, looking around. "One could almost see Ireland from here, do you think?"

I close my eyes for a second and when I open them something has changed. We are now in a great hall. It has high lancet windows, filled with coloured glass and the sun shines in, on shafts of rainbow light. I am sitting at a high table, sitting in the centre, where Papa would sit. Before me there is an array of golden plate, bowls, fruit and candles. My head feels tight. I reach up and find cool metal lays upon it. Am I wearing a crown?

I look around. Kathryn is still there, now dressed in lavender silk, her hair bound up with ribbon, a true lady. John is at her side, his doublet made of blue damask. Music is playing. Mama and Papa are dancing, everyone is watching, and applauding them. Papa does not have his crown on, it that what I am wearing? Have I taken his crown? Mama looks beautiful and never takes her eyes off Papa's face as they pass each other in the dance. I am fascinated by how splendid they look. I cannot look away. They are holding hands. Papa's coronation ring catches the light and I look at my own hand. I wear the same ring, on the finger where the gold band of my investiture ring usually sits. How can that be?

I want the dance to end so I can speak to them. Ask them where we are. Kathryn leans towards me, her lips close to my ear.

"He wanted you to be king, my lamb! Above everything. He wanted you to be king!"

I can smell violets and I look up. Lady Desmond is standing behind John, her hand on his shoulder, tears streaming down her face. She wears a gold ring too, inset with a dark red stone. It looks like blood and I shudder. My head begins to feel light.

A young page puts a platter of meat before me, steaming hot. Another steps up, grinning, he is wearing green and white motley, like a jester. He pours sauce over the meat. Red and thick and I begin to feel sick. I can taste it in my throat. My chest is tight. I don't want to eat it; I have eaten enough. I am too hot. The candles must be burning me. All I want is for the dance to end, for Mama and Papa to come to talk to me. To give Papa his crown back, but my hand begins to shake. No, please! Not now! Not in front of all of these people...!

My body heaves and I retch, leaning over into the bowl. Foul liquid burns the back of my throat. It stings! I feel Mistress Idley's cool hand on my brow. The room is dark. I must have slept all day. I can hear voices, but they are just whispers.

"Shall I tell the king?" It sounds like Sir John. No one answers him. I bend over double again, pain shooting through my stomach. But nothing comes up. I am glad. It hurts too much. I fall back onto my pillows. I knew the meat would be too rich for me. I should have refused it. Told the servants to go away. Has Papa finished dancing yet? I need to speak to him.

"Papa?" my voice is hoarse. My throat is sore. Every bit of me aches. I can even feel the ring on my finger, as if my hand itself is swollen.

"Hush, now, Edward." Mistress Idley puts something cold and damp on my head. Is Kathryn here? That is what she does. When she calls me her lamb.

"We should bleed him..." Someone I cannot recall says. I know the voice. It is... No, I cannot remember.

"No!" Mistress Idley. A hushed warning. "Enough now. Let him be!"

"I will fetch Father Doggett."

I have missed Mass. I must get up. Only everything is too difficult. My arms and legs are like lead. There are pains in my head. Behind my eyes. I cannot even open them. Maybe I should just sleep. Sleep until the morning. Then I will feel better. Then I will go to Nottingham, to the big castle on the hill.

"Papa? Can I come?" I think I hear the words. I am not sure. My throat is dry. I feel someone sit on the bed and put their arms around me, cradling me in a soft embrace. I can smell soap and thyme. But it is not Mama. She always smells of flowers. Summer flowers.

"Ssh, my little lord," Mistress Idley says. Or is it Mama? I am not sure. I want to see her, but I just want to sleep. I always feel better after I have slept. And if I go to sleep quickly, Kathryn may still be there, on the hill. Waiting.

I can feel something moist on my cheek, like rain drops. I hear voices, softer now. Musical words... someone is praying. Their words follow me down into the dark.

The Cross
November 1499

"Do you think it will snow?"

My husband looks back at me and he knows I care for nothing about the weather. He does not speak, for what would he say? I should be proud of him. And I am. Knight of the Garter, a commander in the recent war against the Scottish rebels. He is well thought of by the king. A fellow Welshman. None of what will happen here today is his fault. We have two children, and my belly quickens once again. Two sons, we have. Two boys.

I turn away from him and look at the river. Cold and sluggish, like the blood that runs through my veins. Two boys. I am glad that my sons are home and safe. For is anyone truly safe these days? How long is it since anyone felt secure? That they knew how the path of their life was fixed and where each step along the way would take them. I thought I did once. For a while. A very short while only.

I do not want to think about today, and I do not want to think about the past, so what can I do? I have not seen my brother since he was taken away into the depths of the very palace where we now sit, waiting. I heard he was paraded through the streets some years ago. When Yorkist rebels rose up against the man who had killed their king. Yet, these were people I knew, not traitors. Faces swim before my eyes.

Lord Lovell. Lord Lincoln. Two brave men. Yet there is another I dare not summon up, and I am glad that I do not see his face too. I hear too much of what happened to him, of the sort of man he was, and with the truth of his death there are so many cruel lies.

But I keep my own counsel. It is a skill I learned as a young girl, and one which has served me well. I cleave to it more than ever now. Like a motto.

Should I have spoken up? Have I been wrong to bear the mantle I took up so long ago? Even my husband does not know. I shared my secret with no-one, but there is someone else. A person who knows the truth as surely as I do. I have seen it in her eyes, when she does not know I am looking.

My cousin Bess, now a queen. She knows the man who will be led out to his death today is her brother. But she too keeps her own counsel. I do not blame her. For to recognise her brother would be to damn her own children, and who could do that? Truly?

Many years have passed by. Whispers in a darkened passage. Did I really ever hear them? Of a boy abroad. A boy sent away for his own safety and the peace of the realm.

Dear God, I am being pulled back into the past and it is a place I fear to go! For to see my brother's innocent, smiling face there is just too much to bear today. Not today. I may be able to remember that later, in a few months. But not today.

So I remember others, but they do nothing to lift my leaden heart. King Edward, bright as the sun, always laughing. His ice cool queen, Elizabeth, forever disdainful. My grandmother, her spine forged with a determined, rigid will. My cousin Edward, whom I met only once and very briefly in the city of York. One minute resplendent in cloth-of-gold and jewels, the next, dead of a fever. Poor, frail Queen Anne, coughing her way to an early grave. A king's bastard children, the flame haired Kathryn, the darkly handsome John. A strange stirring makes itself felt, deep inside me. I turn back to my husband.

"Richard?" He looks up, from where he has been staring morosely into the fire. "Do you know where the Gloucester boy was buried?"

His eyes narrow. I have never spoken of this before, but today it should be no surprise. Apart from the fact that I never talk of these things at all.

"The usurper's bastard?" I try not to flinch. It still hurts. Poor John. I am as sure that our Lady is merciful as I am that John did nothing to act against the king. He didn't have to. He had York blood. That was crime enough to seal his fate. I shiver, pulling my shawl around my shoulders. The Tower always was as icy as a tomb, even on the warmest days.

My husband shrugs.

"Where all traitors end up, I would imagine. With the Austin Friars."

I cannot swallow, my throat is almost closed.

"Will Ned...?" He regards me carefully. I forget how close he is to the king. "I would like my brother to rest with my family. At Bisham."

He turns away from me, back to the flames.

"It will need a petition to the king."

"Is it not too late?"

He fiddles with the cuff of his sleeve. He looks embarrassed.

"I have already interceded on your behalf. I am waiting to hear his decision."

My heart softens in thanks. I manage a half-smile which he returns before setting his gaze back upon the fire. I wonder what he is thinking, but dare not ask. It is perhaps better, today, that we say less rather than more. I desperately want to know if he has also asked if the king would consider a pardon. But I do not think my husband would have gone that far. My brother is Plantagenet blood. Part of the male line of the House of York. But then, my sons also hold part of that lineage! Will they be in danger too? How, then, do we keep them safe from harm as they grow into men with their own views and ambitions?

It frightens me. Perhaps, had I been born a boy, I would share my brother's fate. Is Henry so afeared of how he came to the throne that he would remove every single person who he may see as a threat to his dynasty?

But then - maybe he is right.

For today, in executing a young man who has admitted that he may not be who he once purported to be, the king will finally expunge his biggest threat. In a single stroke he will cause the death of my cousin, Richard, Duke of York, even if he will be laid to rest under another name. I wonder if Henry realises that, or if he really believes he is just disposing of another rebel? Another troublesome pretender. Such as he himself once was. For he knows better than most how one single turn of Fortune's Wheel can turn rebel into royal.

Poor Uncle Richard. I do see him now and the memory is entirely painful. I see his face, careworn by the end. Beset by misfortune. Cast into a paupers grave and still blamed for the death of his nephews, one of whom is shortly to die at his successors hands. Of course, even if Henry knew, and he may know, if Bess has dared to tell him. He would not admit that he is about to murder King Edward's son – for that boy is already dead. Killed by his greedily ambitious uncle. It would not do to overturn that myth, for people may then begin to question if other things they have been told are the truth.

Told by whom, they could ask? Ah, thereby hangs a tale!

I heard it said that Henry ordered a fine tomb for King Richard, to be built in the Greyfriars at Leicester. Ten years too late. It may be yet another tale, this one to show how Henry can be magnanimous in victory. Some say it was only to remind the people of England of their former king, of the king who murdered his nephews. For if this king carried out such a heinous deed, how can one of those nephews be threatening to invade the country! He must be an imposter! Those boys are dead. The king's death in battle proved it. God made him pay for his sin!

He is a clever man, Henry. Cunning. It is not an enviable trait in any man. Yet – still he survives, and my cousin Bess has borne him seven children. He has three sons, it should have been four, but one died earlier this year. A son named Edward.

It seems, just now, an unfortunate name.

How many Edward's have passed? King Edward; Edward his son and heir. Richard's son, away in Middleham. And after today, my own brother.

I know that Uncle Richard's daughter Kathryn died in childbirth. She was such a free spirit, just thinking of her makes me smile. I remember she would run around barefoot in the gardens at Greenwich, auburn tresses streaming in the sunlight, only to be reprimanded by her husband. Will still thrives, and has remarried. I don't think he ever really loved Kathryn, nor her him. I don't know why; it is just something I sensed between them. Maybe they would have grown to be fond of each other, had she not passed away, trying to bear him a child.

My thoughts jar as the door swings open and a guard in scarlet livery steps inside. The 'Tudor' rose is emblazoned on his breast. The flower of my own house swallowed by a wild, red dog-rose, its thorns sharp as claws, digging in deep. Or so it seems to me. But I keep my own counsel.

The guard ignores me and walks over to my husband, holding out a letter for him to take. Richard glances at me anxiously, before taking the missive from his hand. The guard steps back a pace, but does not leave. His face is dour. Like the day.

I feel sick. Nauseous. Hopeful. All at the same time.

Richard cracks the blood-red wax, unfolds the letter. Reads it quickly.

"Wait outside." His command to the guard is swift and authoritative. The man obeys without question. I hear Richard sigh heavily and he pushes himself up from his chair. I fix his gaze as he walks over to me. I cannot move. Every limb is numb. Dead.

Our Lady, please have mercy! Please let the king pardon my brother! Whatever he did, he would not have understood the consequences. I am sure Henry knows that. I am certain he knows it all too well. My husband clears his throat.

"Within the hour. First the pretender. Then..." He stumbles over his words. He cannot speak my brother's death sentence even if his king has signed it. "The king has mercifully agreed that he can be buried at Bisham. He has also agreed that you may go see him. Now."

I do not hear what he has said. Not properly. I hear the word 'Bisham' and all I can think of are the cold stone of the Warwick family tombs. Should I have asked for him to go to Tewkesbury, with our mother and father? Would Henry have preferred one traitor to be buried with another?

"What about... the boy?" I cannot say his name. Neither his real one nor the one he has assumed.

"As I said. The Friary." I bite my lip, trying to hide it twisting with irony. So Edward's son will rest with Richard's. Both having met the same end, at the hands of the same man. It seems both fitting and tragic at the same time.

He holds out his hand. I stare at it blankly.

"Do you wish to see him?" All I can do is nod. We walk slowly, behind four of Henry's scarlet bodyguard. Does he think I may try to help Edward escape?

We leave the White Tower and cross the green. The wind is cold, biting. I try not to look to where the block has been set. The raised platform, giving all the best view possible of the king's justice being enacted.

We are led to the Wakefield Tower, and wait outside as the heavy door is unlocked, the thick metal keys jangling like my nerves. The door opens, and I peer inside. It is not dark, but somehow I cannot see. I step over the threshold, alone. The door closes behind me.

There is a bed, linen neatly stretched and tucked in. I see a stool. A small table by the window. There are no books, just a small wooden goblet and a pewter flagon. It is all remarkably sparse, if clean.

"Maggie?" A tremulous voice from behind me and I turn. Dear God, was he hiding behind the door?

I have not seen him in many a year, in fourteen years. But I know him. I know his face as well as my own. I have a vague memory of my father. I feel he looks like him.

I want to cry. I want tears to fill my eyes but they don't. They stubbornly sit in my throat and make it hurt, make it hard to speak. Instead I give a pathetic smile and hold out my hands.

This is not enough for him. He always was an affectionate child, and he lunges forward and embraces me in slim, fragile arms. He smells of soap. Someone has allowed him to bathe? We step back, looking at each other, the same height now, where once he was so small. His head leaning into my skirts. My hand on his silky hair.

He is smiling, his hazel eyes shine, his hair is now a tawny gold. He is clean-shaven, an old scar mars his cheek. I don't remember it being there. His hose are remarkably clean as is his linen shirt, which lays loose around his throat. A glimpse of hair there. He is a man. My brother the child is already gone and I did not see him leave.

"Maggie, is it really you?"

We still stand, hand-fasted. Like lovers. His hands are slim and cool.

"Yes, Ned. It is me." I don't know what to say. So many years, so many things I do not know if he knows or even understands. He is a stranger. He is my brother. "Are you well?"

A question I would ask an acquaintance.

His brows pucker, as if pulled with a thread. He sighs, his eyes move to look out of the window. It occurs to me that I had never been told in what place he had been held within the tower walls. I think this room is not where he has spent the past fourteen years. It is too clean, too well kept. It could appear that he has been prepared. Knowing that he will soon face the curious eyes of the city.

'*Look how well he has been cared for,*' they may grumble. '*Yet still he betrayed his king.*'

I silently rebuke myself for this sudden flight of fancy. I am no longer a child. I should not imagine such things. But still...

"They say I have committed treason."

"I know." The words come out through a throat which is almost too narrow to draw breath.

He seems genuinely perplexed and looks at me again, his eyes full of concern.

"I don't understand. I was talking. Talking to my cousin Richard. He told me how he lived in Burgundy, how Uncle Richard made sure he was safe. How there were people outside who will rescue him and put him on his father's throne."

I am aware that there are ears listening at the door. I swallow, and force myself to answer him. It is agony.

"He is not our cousin, Ned. He... is a trickster. A false person. He could never have done the things he said." But he will not be assured. The creases in his brow grow deeper.

"He would let me out of here and I would be beside him. I would be Warwick. Like our grandfather was. We talked." His voice faded, growing softer. "It was good to have someone to talk to."

His hand rises to his throat, and pulls out something from inside his shirt, curling his fingers around it. It hangs on a leather cord. I think of the ring which sits in my jewellery casket. A present from a king, many Christmases past. "They say I will die for it." He swallows, and I see his throat move awkwardly.

"Yes Ned." I cannot think of what else to say. His hand drops away and reveals what it formerly enclosed. A small, ornately carved wooden cross, and I know it is his own work. I reach up and touch it gently.

"Do you like it?" he asks shyly. He is a child again and my heart bleeds with hurt. All I can do for a moment is nod, still trying to maintain my smile. My knees are beginning to shake beneath my skirts. "I could not have a knife, but I had pieces of stone, of flint, and I sharpened them. I cut a piece of wood from my bed. One of the guards gave me the leather from his jerkin." He stopped, thinking. "He has gone now."

"It is beautiful," I whisper, words catching in my throat, my fingers tracing the ornate carving in the wood. The figure of Christ, embedded within the cross itself. "You always were very gifted."

He smiles as if I have given him the best present in the world and reaches for my hand.

"Do you still have it?"

Before I can react, he has my fingers captured in his and he has his answer. Still held fast on the black velvet ribbon, the small, wooden barrel, now faded from years of exposure to wind and sun. And my skin. He rolls it between his fingers, suddenly troubled. Before I react he has dropped my hand, and reaches up to his neck again

"You should have this."

"No!" I cry out in protest. "No Ned! It is yours. You need it now more than I. Please, you must keep it. You must take it with you. Hold on tight to it, and say your prayers. Pray for all of us."

He looks puzzled for a moment. Once again he is eight years old.

"When the guards come?"

I cannot bear it. I want to take him out of here. Lead him away from his fate. Take him home and take care of him. I would go down on my knees to Henry, tear at my hair and swear on my own children's life that he will never transgress again. That he will be loyal and true. That he has nothing to fear from this Plantagenet prince. But it is too late. Far too late.

"Yes," I say quietly, taking his hands back in mine. "And when the priest comes. You will need it then." He looks towards the window again; his face remarkably calm. I wonder if he really understands what is to happen to him. It should be a blessing that he is in such a state of grace, so why does my heart ache so?

"Will there be people there? Uncle Richard, and John?"

I cannot breathe. It hurts too much. My throat is raw with agony. This is a torture far worse than I could ever have imagined.

"They will be there, Ned. Afterwards. They will be waiting for you. Do not be frightened."

I clasp his hands again and he looks down at my fingers. At the small barrel swinging on its ribbon. I look at his face, so handsome, fair and young. His life wasted, his future gone. Then the cross around his neck catches my eye once again. A vision of him sitting, night after night by the light of a candle, whittling away at a piece of wood. Taking great care, blowing away the dust of his efforts. One detached part of my mind warns me to make sure that the cross is with him when he is buried. If I can.

"I haven't seen them for a long time," he says, his voice expressionless. "It will be good to see them again." His eyes wander back to the window. He seems to get comfort from the daylight. I fear that he may have been a long time in the shadows, but I force the thought down. "I do love Uncle Richard so. He was very kind to me. I am sure he did not mean to keep me here. I told cousin Richard the same. He only did it to keep us safe."

"It was not Uncle Richard, Ned," I reply feebly, but I don't think he hears me. Or can make sense of it.

"Oh," he sighs as if it no longer matters. "Yes, I remember. I remember now. It was a long time ago."

There is a rap on the door. The key turns in the lock once more and I know I must leave.

His eyes fly to the sound, alert now. I reach up and cup his chin with my fingers, turn his face back towards mine.

"God be with you, Edward. Be brave. I will pray for you every day." I think there are tears in his eyes but I cannot be sure. It may just be the reflection of mine. His bottom lip trembles, just a little.

"Can you not stay? Can you come with me? I have missed you, Maggie. Please don't leave!"

His fingers grip mine tightly, so tight I could gasp with pain. He has the power of a man in his grip, although he still seems like a boy.

"Time's up!" The voice behind me is gruff. Determined. I raise his hands to my lips and kiss his fingers.

"Goodbye, Edward." I try to release my hands but he will not loosen his grip. It just grows tighter as his eyes bore into mine, willing me to remain. Oh God, please let this end! Which it does. The guard moves between us.

"Come now, lad. Let the lady go!" His voice is quiet, but commanding and my fingers are suddenly free. Edward turns his back on me, and walks to the window. I want to go and embrace him one more time, but the guard remains at my side. I watch as my brother leans forwards, straining towards the glass.

"I can see him! Is that our cousin Richard?"

I fly from the room as if all the devils of hell are at my heels and fling myself into my husband's arms.

Epilogue

In the end, another week passed before Edward was beheaded. A week after my cousin Richard was hanged at Tyburn, no block in the tower precincts for him. Dragged on a hurdle before jeering crowds, hoisted up by his neck until the life choked out of his body. A fitting end for a traitor from the Lowlands. But... not for the son of a king of England. Henry knows this. So does Bess.

It is a week I spent in prayer and fervent hope that the king would relent, once he ensured my cousin had been safely departed from this world. Once no one said a word. Made a murmur. That there was no dissent from the kings who had courted and promoted him as the White Rose of England. No rebuke from Burgundy, France, Ireland or Scotland. None at all. But Edward's fate was already sealed. Sealed on a bargain, on the assurance of a Spanish marriage for Henry's eldest son.

Richard has just handed me a small, stained, piece of linen. Wrapped inside it is Edward's cross. The figure of Christ now ingrained with his blood, a sign of his own holy trials. I wanted it to go into his grave with him, but in the end my selfish will overwhelmed me. It is all that I have of him. Of the family I once had.

I wrap the cross back inside the linen and lay it in my lap. It will go into my casket with the ring he was never destined to wear. My idle fingers stray to the small, smooth barrel at my wrist, and take comfort from its presence. The last remnant of my past has gone. The faces, and voices will dim in my mind, even as the memories stay, making themselves felt from time to time as bursts of sunlight from behind silvered clouds.

All the flowers of the garden of York are dead now. Wilted and shriveled. Blown away like dust. There are only my own children, and we have shown our loyalty to the Tudor cause. It could be said we have given blood for it. I curl my fingers back around the wooden cross, remember my brother and pray that it is enough.

AUTHOR'S NOTES

Kathryn (or Katherine) Plantagenet, John Plantagenet, Edward of Middleham, Edward, Earl of Warwick. Also, Warwick's elder sister, Margaret. Five children who lived and breathed as we did, in different times, each one of them to suffer a tragic end. Even Margaret, who made it well into maturity, for a while seeming to escape the ominous shadow that stalked the children of York after August 1485.

I had no plan to write this short book, no plan at all. In fact, my head was already somewhere else, in my book outlining the events of Desmond's Daughter, from the perspective of Francis Lovell. Then, a friend asked me to supply some research material for her daughter who is writing an A Level project on the 'Princes in the Tower." As I did this, I thought of someone else held in that Tower. Someone whose fate is also something of a mystery. Someone who in no way shares the fascination surrounding his missing cousins.

From that thought came "The Innocent,' for surely of anything else, this is something that can be truly said of John. His only crime was to be born Richard's son and to still be alive after his father was killed. From there, the other stories came thick and fast. Four snapshots of their lives in happier times, and four where they were unable to escape their fate. All died young. Even the eldest, at twenty four, was said to be as simple as a child.

That these children lived, and died, is fact. As is the truth that of those who died young, we only know the exact date of birth and death of Edward, George Plantagenet's son. He was executed for treason in 1499 – one week after the execution of 'Perkin Warbeck.' These deaths freed up the possibility of a marriage for Henry Tudor's eldest son to Catherine of Aragon, who later was to be treated so dreadfully by Henry VIII. Edward's sister Margaret survived, serving as governess to Princess Mary before eventually becoming a victim to Henry's increasing vindictiveness. She was executed in 1541 at the age of sixty seven. Like his father before him, Henry did not turn a hair at expunging anyone with a drop of Plantagenet blood. Or any blood really.

Edward of Middleham, Richard's son, died at Middleham Castle in April of 1484. There is no record of exactly when he died or what he died of, but it is thought that he was a frail child. Recent research seems to pin his death to around the 18th April, and not the 9th as so often reported. This date is often used as a 'divine intervention' as this was also the date upon which King Edward IV died, just one year earlier. Linking the dates in this way, incorrect though it was, allows more perpetuation of Tudor mythology. Of a vengeful God, reaping retribution on King Richard for his sins.

In writing the story of Edward, I began to reflect on the young boy himself, and wonder if he did suffer from some debilitating ailment. To my knowledge, he was only seen outside of Middleham Castle once, at York Minster in 1483. He was never brought to London. There is little on record about him other than his wardrobe accounts, his investiture and gifts sent to him by the good citizens of York. The young boy seemed to be very well protected from the outside world, and I have only just begun to consider why this may be.

Richard's illegitimate children are shadowy figures. Their mother, or mothers, are unknown (for continuity here I have linked these stories in with my novel 'Desmond's Daughter') as the actual dates and years of their birth. What is certain is that the were the issue of encounters before Richard married Anne Neville. He both acknowledged and cared for them, as he did in later years for Edward of Warwick, which shows the true nature of the man with regard to his care for the welfare of children. One has to wonder if the experiences he suffered in his own unsettled childhood led him to act in this way. This would also give credence to the fact that at least one of King Edward's sons could have been sent abroad to keep him safe, as Richard himself was when he was very young and the country was in turmoil.

Kathryn (or Katherine) was eventually given in marriage to William Herbert, Earl of Huntingdon, and may have made her home at Raglan Castle, for a short time at least. She is thought to be dead by 1487 when William is described as being a 'widow.' It is possible she died in childbirth or of the sweating sickness, a virulent disease which swept the country, some said having been brought into England by Henry Tudor's French mercenary army. There is some compelling evidence to suggest that she may have been buried in the church of St James Garlickhythe in London.

John (John of Gloucester or John of Pomfret/Pontefract) was Richard's son. We know he was knighted at York in 1483 and was made Captain of Calais in March 1485. His eventual fate is unknown, but here I rely on the account that he was probably executed for treasonous correspondence with Ireland. He may have been executed at any time after 1485, and there is a record of Henry VII paying him a pension of £20 per annum, but it is not clear how long this was paid for. It is also likely that he was executed at the time when Henry was worried about the invasion by the boy later known as 'Perkin Warbeck' – who many supported as Richard, Duke of York, and the rightful claimant to the throne of England, based on the English king's reversal of the 'Titulus Regis.' This would make his execution anywhere between 1494 and 1499 when Buck states that "there was a base son of King Richard III made away, and secretly, having been kept long before in prison." For dramatic licence, I have pulled in this date significantly to 1487. I somehow feel that if he had still been alive at this time, Henry would have found a way to pull him into the alleged conspiracy which took place between Warwick and Warbeck. He could then have dispatched him quite openly and with just cause, at least in his eyes.

After all, no one knows. Like the fate of two other York princes, despite endless speculation, no one really knows.

It did occur to me that I could have included those very two Princes, Edward and Richard, in this short collection, but I dismissed that as soon as it arose. I think there has already been enough light shed on what is known, and indeed what is NOT known and until something new is found, I am happy to leave that subject be.

Printed in Poland
by Amazon Fulfillment
Poland Sp. z o.o., Wrocław